P9-AOK-259

COMING ATTRACTIONS

Dayv James-French, Lesley Krueger & Rohinton Mistry

4

Acknowledgements: "Domestic Order" by Dayv James-French first appeared in *antioch review.* "Victims of Gravity" by Dayv James-French was originally published in *Grain* under the title "Wild Kingdom." "Lend Me Your Light" by Rohinton Mistry was first published in *The Toronto South Asian Review.* "Condolence Visit" by Rohinton Mistry originally appeared in *Canadian Fiction Magazine* and "The Collectors" by Rohinton Mistry was first published in *Malahat Review.*

ISBN 0 88750 640 2 (hardcover)
ISBN 0 88750 641 0 (softcover)

Cover art by Maxwell Bates
Book design by Michael Macklem

Printed in Canada

PUBLISHED IN CANADA BY OBERON PRESS

An executive of an American corporation has threatened a "scorched earth" policy if Gulf and Western's plans for a Canadian publishing affiliate are tampered with.

We await the sound of helicopters, the smell of napalm.

The government has announced that in the trade negotiations with the U.S., Canadian culture is not for sale, although all cultural matters will be on the bargaining table.

There used to be a naughty expression for women who took that attitude to sex.

Still.

People magazine has discovered Robertson Davies.

Everyone has discovered Margaret Atwood.

We still have Peter Gzowski.

And in all corners of the country, men and women are quietly going about the business of trying to create fine and touching and delightful stories.

Editing is a gentle, harmless activity, not unlike gardening, equally apt to be seasonal, equally dependent on the benignity of the universe.

Each fall, in *Coming Attractions,* the editors offer a group of three stories each by three new writers whose work has given us pleasure. Between sales and library borrowings, the stories will eventually reach a small community of readers. The book will not be mentioned during Question Period in the House of Commons. It will not likely raise the ire of Gulf and Western. But for some readers, the talent and inspiration and hard work of the writers will find an echo, and our pleasure in the discovery of the stories will be shared.

Three young writers.

Dayv James-French was born on P.E.I. in 1958 and has lived in various parts of Canada, as well as Tel Aviv. He took a degree in religion at Carleton University and then went on to study creative writing at the University of Victoria. He has worked at a number of unlikely jobs and currently does occasional work in educational testing.

Of how he came to writing, he says: "I was reading before I started kindergarten (my sister was school librarian) and knew that one day I would write, knew this with the same intensity I knew I would smoke, heavily. Doing both meant 'adult' without the messy process of 'growing up.'"

The characters in his stories may be seen as struggling with the difficult choice between being "adult" or only "grown up." His titles, "Domestic Order," "Signals" and "Victims of Gravity" suggest this kind of struggle; the need to make sense of things without being merely sensible. His young men, thoroughly proper on the surface, exist in a state of internal exile. They are like clever children determined to spell the word "love" while equipped with an alphabet that lacks the appropriate letters.

Rohinton Mistry was born in Bombay in 1952. He immigrated to Toronto in 1975, a part of that Indian diaspora that is having an increasing effect on literature all over the world—think of V. S. Naipaul, Salman Rushdie, Bharati Mukherjee. For ten years, until 1985, Mistry worked in a bank, and from 1978 to 1984 he attended evening classes at the University of Toronto, studying for a BA in English and philosophy. In 1983 he saw the announcement of a Hart House literary contest, wrote his first short story to enter and won first prize. The next year he won again, and since publishing a number of stories and receiving an Explorations Grant from the Canada Council, he has quit his bank job to write full time.

Rohinton Mistry's stories are immediately intriguing for their evocation of the life of the Parsee community of Bombay, but what is most remarkable about his work is his sense of character, the intricacy and fullness with which his people come alive in their world. The loving, triumphant Daulat, the unfortunate Dr. Moday take on a firm and vibrant existence in the reader's mind.

Lesley Krueger was born in 1954 in Vancouver. She studied political science at the University of British Columbia but never graduated. Like Dayv James-French she was always aware of wanting to write, but having been warned there was no money in it she trained herself as a journalist, worked for the Toronto *Star* and the Vancouver *Sun*, travelled for a year in Europe and Asia and ended up in Toronto as a producer for the CBC's "As It Happens." She later worked as a freelancer for CBC and *Maclean's*. Through all this time she was writing, and her first publication was a story in *Tamarack Review*.

She began writing full time while her husband was holder of a Nieman Fellowship at Harvard, and the stories in this book were written during that year and during the year following in Toronto. She is currently living with her husband and son in Mexico City.

The world of Lesley Krueger's stories is a wide-ranging and complicated one where things never go in only one direction. Just what kind of man is the photojournalist in "Ban Mai"? Why does the father in "Miracles" no longer speak? We're never given a simple answer. The stories have an abundance of detail, a weight of perception, but the more the surface of the world is observed, the more mysterious it seems. The mysterious is too often seen as mere evasion of facts; the power of Lesley Krueger's stories is in their combination of articulation and mystery.

DAVID HELWIG

Dayv James-French

Domestic Order

Ken keeps his eyes focused on a spot about the size of a host, consecrated or not, on his father's chest: the suction pad of the cardiac monitor. During his last complete physical, Ken lay on a cold metal table with these clinging to his own chest, his upper arms, his calves, their slight tugging exactly the sensation of being nibbled by fish.

Sympathetic goosebumps had broken out on his flesh and he imagined his lips turning blue, his mother's voice calling him from the lake. He would be eleven in this memory, standing knee-deep in the water, looking down at his feet on the silt bottom, unable to lean forward into the most rudimentary dog paddle. That winter he was signed up for swimming lessons after school—sometimes his wet hair would freeze into a sharp bear claw against the back of his neck as he waited for the bus home—and the following spring the instructor from the Y, and Ken's mother, moved to another town. Ken never conquered his fear, of water closing over his head. He was afraid he would be effaced.

"Could you spell your last name for me?" the technician had asked. Since his surname is not a difficult one, Ken assumed he was being given a rote task to put him at ease, to keep the EKG from recording the indulgence of mortal speculation rather than the placid pumping of his everyday heart. "Capital em," he started, and rhymed off the letters in a sing-song. To his surprise, the tehnician copied this down, and he realized she had needed the information. There was no deeper purpose. He, once again, had read too much into the situation.

The oxygen tent is made of a plastic about six times the thickness of a dry-cleaning bag. Through this, his father's skin has the hazy cast of meat with freezer burn. Meat wrapped in plastic sweats and loses all its moisture; this is something Ken knows: aluminum foil is best for long-term preservation. He considers the logistics of getting his father into pyjamas. The man always wore these at home, and kept his slippers at the side of the bed precisely where his feet would touch down in case of a fire. Domestic order is everything.

In the silence of Intensive Care, the tent makes an icy, crackling sound. "The nurse says you're comfortable," Ken whispers in the direction of his father's chest. The bed is cranked up to prevent fluid collection in the lungs. Ken thinks of doughnuts dunked in coffee, the sacs and pockets of air filling with liquid, the spreading stain as the doughy connecting tissue is saturated. They would be almost eye-to-eye, he and his father, if he turned. He puts his hands deep into his pockets and, louder, adds, "I don't know how they can tell a thing like that. I guess it's relative."

"Your son is visiting," the day nurse says from the doorway. Earlier, in the hall, Ken had hesitated to make any assumptions and checked the man's plastic name bar for professional initials. A white costume could mean anything. The man might have been, even, a barber, hired to spruce up the critical cases. But Julian Snuggs is an RN. His voice is loud and artificially bright, like a movie soundtrack in the afternoon when the volume hasn't been turned down to compensate for the hollowness of a nearly empty theatre. "Has he said 'hello'?"

Ken looks up at his father's face, where a thick X of white adhesive tape marks the goal of a clear plastic tube. An end of this, or another tube entirely, curves up between his eyebrows, a horn more transparent than fingernails, capped by a threaded yellow button. An entry? An exit? It looks careless, the second tube, like something dangling from a dresser drawer after a hasty clean-up. His father's eyes are open and empty, devoid of expression. What looks troubled and thoughtful is merely the reflection of the room's window. Thin grey clouds are weaving over the sky, promising rain. It's Thanksgiving. The tent crackles up and falls.

"Can he talk?" Ken asks, without turning his head, hardly moving his lips, the way the uncomfortably rich address the hired help. There is no pleasure in counting on the paid kindness of strangers.

"Not speech, with the tube," the nurse says. "But he could show that he knows you're here. Has he done that?"

Ken grips the chrome crib-rail of the narrow bed and rocks back on his heels as if preparing to climb up onto the mattress; a six-year-old, bored with the Saturday cartoons and wanting Daddy's attention. It seems to him, now, he's been doing this his whole life. He puts his hands back into his pockets. He can lose awareness of them—his hands and feet—where they are in relation to the rest of his body. One night he had awakened with a cold, cold hand touching his face. His own hand, it turned out, numbed by the weight of his head held awkwardly in the V of his arm; but for a moment he had thought, "Time's up," and came close to humiliating himself.

"My brother will be here later this afternoon," he says.

"Won't that be nice," Julian says. He folds the tent back under itself, across the man's chest, and raises the arm where a network of veins map to a border of white—more adhesive tape—and emerge as a clear tunnel to a suspended bottle. The sheet falls back and Ken is staring at his father's cock, thumbing from a Brillo tangle of greyed hair. The circumcision ridge is a leathery brown. With a practised flip, Julian returns the sheet and smoothes it down.

So, Ken thinks. Now I know.

Guilty, he looks away, to the cardiac monitor where a line as pale and ephemeral as cigarette smoke suddenly spikes across the cathode tube. What excitement of the heart is being traced? Even here, there can be secrets. The machines are godless; they know nothing immaterial.

"I'll have to come back in a few minutes, to do an irrigation," Julian says. Ken feels obligated to pretend he understands this, and nods his acceptance. "But you can visit until then. It's important for him to stay aware of his surroundings."

"Sure, I'll stay," Ken agrees. His voice has risen, in pitch and volume, to match the nurse's. Overheard, they might be old friends, reunited and attempting to dismiss their new environment, more comfortable in the smooth geography of their memories.

He waits for the nurse to leave, gives him time to get down the hall away from the room. Carefully lifting the side of the oxygen tent, exposing the side of his father's head, he bends so his lips are close to the man's ear and hisses, "Damn you. You don't even know I'm here. Damn you to hell." He replaces the plastic, trapping the invisible gas, and leaves the room without turning back. The harsh lighting and slick tile of the hospital corridor remind him of an airport. People come and go.

The estranged wife of a politician has been given an afternoon television talk show. Her guest today is Dr. Wilhelm Bark, president of Surgeons for Survival, a nuclear-protest group. The woman is more celebrated for her estrangement than for her marriage; the doctor has achieved prominence because an evil world tilts on the edge of destruction. Everybody is a star.

"Dr. Bark," the woman starts, with a cosily familiar tone. Ken imagines they met moments before the taping. One of them would have held a cardboard cup of synthetically whitened coffee. It's not possible the show is done live; the politician would have influence as well as a limit to personal embarrassment. "Thermonuclear war produces a great deal of heat, does it not?"

"Well, yes," the doctor says. He swings his body forward on the swivel chair, as if he needs the momentum to pitch a whole paragraph.

"I suppose," the woman interrupts, anxious to score her own points. It's her show, after all. "A cream- or water-based blush would stand up better than a powder blush-on."

Ken's hoot could have come from the doctor's dropped-open mouth. "There's perspective for you. And I thought I didn't watch afternoon television because it was vulgar." He reaches forward to snap off the Sony. His laugh was too loud. His father's hospitalization has made the day a solemn occasion; location has nothing to do with it. Even in his own home, he feels deference is expected of him. To whatever power might be attending, his father's claim is greater. Ken shouldn't call attention to himself.

"What? Am I missing something?" Tony calls from the bathroom.

"Nothing. Never mind." Ken raises his voice so his brother can hear him through the closed door. He's smoking up in there. "Smoking out," Ken calls it, disliking the clubbiness of stoned people, their attitude that sharing the experience made it authentic. Also, he thinks the actual smoking is messy and unattractive. He remembers having joints explode in his fingers, sending showers of embers down to burn his shirt front. "Wow, seeds," was the correct response when this happened, delivered with an appreciative nodding. Seeds were organic, an earthy, natural element prized by a group of people who had just scarfed down six family-sized bags of Cheez Doodles. For a time, Ken had thought orange lips were a side effect of marijuana. This theory had caused him considerable alarm when he noticed the number of small children evidently on drugs outside the street's 7-11 store. Now he knows better. Some of his friends still smoke in his house—Ken doesn't ask them to respect the difference between a joint or two and the 40 to 50 cigarettes he goes through in a day—but the rules are different for family.

He imagines his father will have been given morphine or Demerol. (He knows these words from a required course in psychopharmacology: his degree is in psychology; he also knows the effect of damage caused by a massive insult to the brain. "Insult to the brain" he reacts to with an emotional and visceral chilling.) For today, at least, drugs will be one more thing for Tony and his father to have in common. Maybe the two of them will giggle and snort, suffixing incomplete statements with "far out" while Ken slowly transforms himself into a piece of the wall. Being fair helps. Ken's hair is, in fact, the colour of aged ecru semi-gloss, his eyes a pale blue almost transparent in some lights.

"All clean," Tony announces, entering the room with his hands held up at chest level, palms facing in. They were raised to the euphemism of excusing themselves to "wash my hands." Their mother, in a family of men, had lost patience with announcements of "gotta take a leak." Ken's private fantasy is that her new husband was attractive to her because, except first thing in the morning, under cover of the running shower, he never used the toilet at home; he pissed in the pool at work. Years after being abandoned, Ken still derives a small pleasure from this mild rudeness.

"Ready to go?" Ken asks. Tony has started a slow orbit of the living-room, picking up things for casual appraisal, putting them back in not quite the right place. "Put that down," Ken cautions of an especially fragile ceramic.

"Well, okay," Tony says. "Don't fuss. Can I put on a record, at least or do you get antsy about other people using anything of yours?"

"Go ahead," Ken says, feeling his brother has narrowly escaped having his hands slapped and willing to be generous. He puts his own hands between his thighs and squeezes his legs closed. "If you think you have time," he adds.

"Lots of time, lots of time," Tony mutters. He's pulling

albums halfway out of the teak stand, checking the titles, sliding them back in. "These are in alphabetical order, aren't they?"

"I'm surprised you could tell," Ken says after a moment, needing the time to separate anger from the prissiness he's been accused of. Tony is in his third year of something called international media, a discipline just under art history and film studies on Ken's hierarchy of useless subjects. Their father had curled his lip at Ken's major. "Just sitting there listening to people making too much of themselves. What kind of thing is that for a man to do? Talk never solved anything." The man was holding a small knife and an orange, his wrists pressed hard against the table's edge to steady his hands, and while he spoke he carefully unwound the skin in a single ribbon that kept the shape of the orange when he put it down on the table. "It's not just talking," Ken said. "It's understanding." He carefully rolled the bright globe into his palm, its cut latitudes marked by the paler insides. Zest of orange, he thought, just as his father said, "It's a Jew thing to do." In Ken's palm the hollow orange was as weightless and vivid as an egg blown and dyed for Easter. Talk never solved anything.

The noisy chewing of the coffee grinder drowns out whatever album Tony has chosen. Ken is comfortable in his own kitchen, playing host. He scoops the coffee, fine as flour, from the grinder and into the paper cone filter, slowly pours simmering water over this. A trick of the wrist, the correct pouring technique. While the coffee drips, he puts two mugs and a small pitcher of cream on a plastic tray stamped with a map of the London subway system. He had driven a rented car, on his last holiday, south from London, to Salisbury, to Clovelly, to Land's End. At Glastonbury, Ken walked around the brick outline of the abbey that had once stood there. Only sections of the wall remained, like a theatrical set, the rest dismantled, the stone carted away. The grass under his feet was very green. The brick was grey. Ken looked up, at a leafy tree in the middle distance. A bird cut across his peripheral vision, right at that moment, and disappeared in the sky. Ken looked at his feet again, and understood that King Arthur was buried there. Nobody made this up. He could have left, walked away at any speed, and this would not change. King Arthur. At that moment, Ken knew the mechanism of history: what was, is.

He bends slightly, his elbows on the Formica counter, to examine his face in the chrome side of the toaster: clear skin, nose a bit round at the end, good upper teeth. Turning his head, straining his eyes to see himself in profile, he grimaces, pulling his lower lip down from his teeth, tautening the jaw and chin line he shares with Tony. They are, visibly, brothers; sons of the same father. He lets his face slacken, the crescent of skin where neck meets face creased from too many nights of reading in bed, his head nearly parallel with the book in his lap, almost perpendicular to his body.

Lifting the plastic filter holder from the top of the coffee pot, he swings this over the sink, one palm cupped to catch any drips, then places it where it will drain directly into the pipe and not stain the porcelain. He carries the tray up the steps, one, two, to the false floor of the living-room. When he bought the house the original hardwood had been hidden under wall-to-wall avocado pile held down by a few thousand finishing nails. A rented sander was torn up by eight or twelve hundred of these before Ken admitted defeat and built over the floor.

Tony has his back to the room, staring out the window at the light sprinkling of rain. Against the glass, he looks like one of the black cardboard silhouettes in a shooting-gallery. Ken has a flashing, brief image of his brother buckling forward, falling into the room, neatly bent at the waist.

"Coffee's here," he shouts. Then he adds, "Maybe you

could turn that down?" although the Springsteen album—*Nebraska*—is playing well within his own decibel level.

"The neighbours?" Tony suggests, but he moves to adjust the volume, his fingers slender and elegant on the aluminum knob, his calibration of reduction exact.

"No, me." Ken stares at his brother, for just a little longer than it takes to acknowledge the diminished sound, then passes him one of the mugs, already creamed. "You don't take sugar, do you?"

"I don't think I even know anyone who still does." Tony carries his coffee across the room and sits on the bare floor, leaning against the wall between the stereo speakers. He closes his eyes and a tremor ripples his shoulders as a bass note rolls out into the room. "Excellent," he says.

"I think you'd hear it better in front of the speakers," Ken says. His mug is too hot to pick up; he cages his fingers over its rim, the steam rising into his palm, beading into the lines there.

"You be the audience," Tony offers. "I'll be on stage."

"Just like old times."

"What?" Tony opens his eyes, puts his coffee on the floor beside him. "Are you going to start that stuff about your being the whipping boy so I could have an idyllic childhood? Are you?"

"I wasn't planning to." Ken takes an eye-watering sip of his coffee, reaches for a cigarette, lights it, then coughs into his fist.

"You know what I was thinking about, when I was in your john? Tony the Pony." He says this with the certainty that his brother will know what he's talking about.

"Tony the Pony?" Ken repeats, then remembers, just before Christmas, maybe a dozen years ago, the ads for a half-sized plastic pony, saddled and frozen in a galloping stance. "The real riding pony," a part of the jingle comes back to him. "God, that's going back a bit," he says.

"It's like yesterday," Tony says. "I wanted one of those more than anything in the whole world. More than," he pauses, searching for a standard, "world peace, even."

"That's some wanting." Ken glances at his watch. Even immediate family are barred from Intensive Care at meal-times. It's getting close. He sits, silent, watching his brother. Tony's eyes are closed again. The album ends and the tone arm is raised, mechanically, and swings over to its cradle.

"That *the* bothered me a bit. It should have been apostrophe ess." He draws this in the air with his next-to-little finger. "Tony's pony. It was made for me. I watched TV shows I hated—'Huckleberry Hound,' 'Quick Draw McGraw'—because I knew they'd run the commercial. Finally they arrived at Toyland, maybe six of them, a little corral of Tony's ponies. I may have imagined this part, but each of them had a slightly different expression. One was raring to go, one was a work-horse; the one I wanted was courageous and resourceful. Yup, he was really something."

"The commercials never mentioned the battery," he goes on. "Was I ever that young? It was a big sucker, the size of a car battery." Tony's hands are T-squares, blocking off a measure in the air before him. "You know how Dad was. 'You don't want a toy that spends money.' But I figured even that wasn't insurmountable and I dragged him to Toyland to see it. Tony's pony."

The light from the window is fading, the single lamp at Ken's side is yellow and weak. He can hardly see his brother across the room, at the end of the parallel strips of flooring, his hands and face amorphous.

"Tony?"

"Oh, he made all the right noises, he said it was nice, and I rode one—the work-horse one, not mine—around the floor, while he looked over the book. Warranty? Instructions? I don't know. But he found what he was looking for."

"Yes." Ken agrees.

"This little print said Tony could carry up to 150 pounds, no more. 'You don't want that,' he said. 'You'll outgrow it by summer, just when you'll want to take it outside.' And that was that. End of discussion."

"You think he should have got it for you?"

"Yes," Tony says. "No, not really. What started this was your bathroom scales. Do you know what I weigh?"

"No."

"One hundred and forty-six pounds. I am 22 years old, five-foot-ten and I weigh 146 pounds."

"And you feel that he lied to you?" Ken suggests. His tone is professional. This is not a small story that he's hearing: his working day is predicated on these perceptions tangling in complex warps and wefts, the stories of his own life are neither greater nor less important.

"I would have ridden off into the sunset," Tony says, or perhaps, "I always wanted to have a pet."

"I'm sorry?" Ken angles his head. There is a low humming from the speakers. The stereo may not be properly grounded. In the manual the leads were red and black; in real life the leads were black and grey. Ken worked on the assumption that the black remained constant. His chances were 50-50.

"I said: So don't tell me."

"I won't," Ken says. The small amount of coffee remaining in his mug is cold. He doesn't remember taking more than the one sip; a kind of automatic pilot must have taken over to deal with such an easy activity, drinking coffee. "What I will tell you is that you've missed visiting time. You're not allowed in for meals. Do you suppose they're messy?"

"What?" Tony asks. Then, "I'm getting hungry myself."

"We could go out. Thanksgiving dinner."

"Tom turkey and all the trimmings? We'd have to go to

the bus station, someplace like that, filled with transients."

"I was thinking of Hoagy Heaven. We can have turkey subs."

"The content without the form," Tony says, and scuttles forward across the floor, pulling himself with his heels toward the sound of Ken's laugh. "Am I funny?"

"That was." Ken is dialling up the rheostat for the overhead lights. Tony covers his eyes dramatically, moaning, "King of the Mole People."

"I'm going to change. Why don't you listen to the other side of the album? Have some more coffee."

Ken stops at the top of the stairs, looking across the hall into his second bedroom: the guest-room, although he's gotten no further in fixing it up than putting in a sagging double bed covered with a dark brown corduroy spread, and a four-drawer, stained maple dresser. The floor of the room is littered with Ken's shoes—Adidas, Clarke's in leather and suede, paper-thin beige Italian loafers, Kodiaks, two pairs of Frye boots—a collection too eclectic to suggest anything at all except, perhaps, costume accessories.

In his own room, he pulls himself across the bed, turns to lie on his back, his ankles crossed, his arms out straight from his shoulders. His hands and feet are suspended over empty space. After the tests at the clinic, for his physical, he had gone to his own doctor's office for the results. His chest X-rays were clipped to a lit viewing-screen, two grey gumdrop-shapes just over the doctor's right shoulder. "Difficulties with motor co-ordination? Speech, use of hands, walking?" the doctor asked, ready to check the appropriate boxes on the Family History form, in the column beside the one where "Maternal" had a ballpoint stroke oblique from left to right. Ken nodded, swallowed, said, "Yes. Yes." Only when he was leaving the office did he ask about the X-rays. "Oh, they're okay. No signs of bronchial malignancies," the doctor said, "yet."

Ken covers his eyes with his forearm. Through the floorboards, faintly, he can hear Springsteen. Tony has turned up the volume again. He rolls off his bed, steps out of his slacks, changes into jeans and pulls a cotton V-neck over his shirt. Carrying a pair of boots taken from the guest-room, he walks down the stairs, carefully, his socks slippery on the varnished wood. Back in the living-room, he notes that Tony has achieved, predictably, the wall-hugging stage of expanded consciousness.

"I shouldn't smoke," Tony says. "It just makes me depressed."

"Does it? Then you're right, you shouldn't." Ken puts his boots beside the couch, takes the tray, his mug, the creamer, crosses to pick up Tony's mug from the floor.

"From now on," Tony raises his hand in a Scout's promise. "Cocaine or amphetamines, only. This album is so sad. It should be faster."

Ken, on his way to the kitchen, turns back. "There's a pitch control on the turntable. You can make it faster."

"Is that what it's for?" Tony smacks his forehead with his palm, whistles a thin, jagged note. "What a feature."

"It's not what it's for, but it'll work. Then we leave, okay?" The question goes unanswered; Tony is bent over the stereo, compromising the speed of sound.

The sidewalk is dry, as if it had never rained. Since he bought a house—is buying his house—Ken has started to notice just how much happens outside of it. He had imagined his universe would become centred, that everything would happen within his own four walls. Instead, it now seems he has to leave home to get experience, excitement, change of any kind. In a single evening he can be two people: the flushed, high-spirited dinner companion; and later the domestic, routine partner, in the tangle of his own sheets, as if his own room contained a marriage bed of habitual boredom, transforming him, transforming her, into a sedate couple of long standing, without surprises. "It's the thrill of the hunt," he mocks himself, to explain away the difference. But, still, he notes the influence of otherness. The neighbourhood itself, he imagines, was zoned by someone with a map at city hall who never visited the actual streets. Three houses up, at the corner, there is a Presbyterian church with a tiny cemetery behind it. Diagonally across the intersection—and here Ken can see the compass point arcing across the map, bisecting the street—a Mr. Muffins bread factory stands behind a chain-link fence, six or eight trucks in permanent residence on several city lots' worth of concrete, lowering property values enough for Ken to be able to afford the street.

His boot heel catches in a section of sidewalk split and raised and he grabs at Tony's arm, his hand clamping just above his brother's elbow. "Cross here," he says.

"Shouldn't I look both ways first?" Tony asks. "Don't be paternal with me."

"Was I?"

"Since I was born. That's the difference between us, you know. You were born middle-aged, and I just wanted to be old enough to take control of my own childhood."

"Is that what you think?" Ken pushes his hands deep into the pockets of his jacket, watches his feet as he steps up onto the curb. He can feel his own smile, and turns to face the road, away from the streetlights.

"I remember exactly one time that you did anything even remotely juvenile." Tony's voice is precise, too exact. Ken remembers taking the train home from college, having smoked until he was "off like Jack the Bear," and being the only passenger able to walk a straight line on the shifting floor, even on a curve. A powerful impetus, the fear of losing control.

"And that was?" he prompts.

You were out some place, late, and I took the top bunk. When you got home you didn't even say anything, just grabbed the bottom sheet and pulled me off, pillow, blankets and all. Dad came running in and dragged you out of the room, remember? I crawled into the lower bunk, imagining you were being whipped to within an inch of your life. And rightly so."

"Tony, no," Ken starts to laugh. "I shouldn't even tell you this, revenge fantasies are important, but it wasn't like that at all. All he did was yell at me."

"Yelling's okay, as long as he put the fear of God into you."

"But he said, he said," Ken stops, holding onto a No Parking sign for support. "He said, 'Your brother could have landed on his head and I don't have time to raise a brain-damaged child.'"

"That's funny?" Tony steps back, the streetlight throwing the bottom of his face into shadow. His eyes are wide open, glistening. Ken gasps, recovering, holds out one hand for forgiveness just as Tony's laugh barks out. "It is, isn't it? It is funny. Oh, God." They clutch at each other, sucking the cool evening air deep into their lungs, helpless for a long time. Finally, they straighten, their breathing shallow and ragged, and continue their walking, careful not to look at each other.

From the sidewalk, they can tell that Hoagy Heaven is closed but, together, they cross the empty parking-lot and stand in front of the window. The only light inside is from the fluorescent tubes of the glass-fronted refrigerators.

"I guess we're out of luck."

"Maybe it's just as well." Tony shields his eyes with his cupped hands, peering in. "Purple and orange vinyl all over the place, in there."

"The hospital cafeteria is red and yellow. It might still be open, you could get something there," Ken suggests.

"I'll get a Pecan Sandie on my way home. I'm not going to the hospital." Tony turns away, takes a few steps, stops and leans against the window. "I've forgotten where the bus stop is," he says, keeping his back to Ken.

"Just past the lights," Ken says.

"I used to know that. Funny, not to remember."

"He might not make it, Tony." Ken isn't sure he's said this out loud until Tony turns, his mouth open, face slack.

"You think I don't know? You don't have to tell me that. But I'm not going to see him. I can't stand sick people. It makes my flesh crawl to think about old people, about disease. Hospitals!" He shakes his head, like a horse cut by its bit, and wipes the back of his hand across his mouth.

"But you're here. And you didn't come home for the holidays." Ken is leaning back, has to move his feet to keep his balance.

"I came because you called me, long distance, at 8:30 in the morning. I know the conventions. That doesn't mean I agree with the sentiment. I did my part, okay? Now I'm going home, to Dad's house; I still have my keys." He turns, and walks quickly away, about six steps, then slows to a normal pace.

Ken looks up at the sky, for the stars in the few constellations he can name, but they are obliterated by the brightness of the night-time city. Denial, he thinks, followed by anger, bargaining, depression. But that is not the order that concerns him. From another part of him, a different sequence presents itself: guilt, confession, penance followed by absolution. Was he, was anyone, ever so young?

"Tony!" His voice is loud on the nearly deserted street. Tony looks back from the corner, where he is waiting for the light to change although there is no apparent traffic. "Tony, even if he dies, it doesn't mean you have to grow up." He watches, just long enough to be able to tell that his brother has heard, and crosses back to his own street, looking down at his boots against the sidewalk, managing to miss some, but not all, of the cracks. He stops beside the Mr. Muffins fence.

He has never smelled the bakery in the daytime, imagining the building was merely a bread factory, housing row after row of plastic-wrapped loaves stacked to the ceiling. The fragrance was obscured by car exhaust, bus fumes, the dry odour like stale talc that rose from the asphalt sidewalks. Now he stands in a warm puff of yeasty redolence and is overwhelmed by images of home: Mother taking fresh bread from the oven; running over the cool green grass, playing in the water sprinkler on a hot afternoon; the squeak of red waggon wheels as the lemonade stand is pulled to the corner bus stop, to catch the commuter trade; the slow pitching and leather slap of ball to glove during a twilight game of catch.

After an extended, longing moment, he realizes that the images in his mind are remembered from television commercials. Such things have never happened in his own life.

Signals

Brian's mother has started watching a lot of television, mostly cops-and-robbers dramas on one of the cable stations, and she's become very specific in her apprehension of a criminal network in the suburb where she lives.

"There was a '78 Dodge van parked across the street all of yesterday afternoon. In front of the old Pinney place? They might be casing the joint."

Brian takes a deep drag from his cigarette, to keep from laughing into the phone. The tone she has adopted, in character with her cynical, vigilante role, is amusing enough to stop him from questioning her belief that evil is external, identifiably *they*. Some residual Catholic confusion surfaces briefly: is his mother's belief heretical? Is his own? He lets this pass unexamined. And politeness alone stops him from questioning her belief that since he's home at 8:30 on a Wednesday evening his time is available to her.

Across the room, Beaver mouths, "Your mother?" and holds up the bottle of scotch. Brian nods, affecting a heavy world-weariness, and raises four fingers pressed together to indicate the size of drink he needs. As Beaver passes, on his way to the kitchen for ice, he runs one hand up the inseam of Brian's jeans, and makes loud kissing noises into the air. Brian covers the mouthpiece with his cigarette hand, making a threatening grimace. But then he pats at Beaver's ass, tight in his own jeans. Mixed signals.

"That's what they do, you know. They learn your hours. They could know when I'm not here and just load up that van with everything I own. The neighbours wouldn't notice a thing."

"Your neighbours? They would so. They'd be over in a flash to make sure those burglars had clean clothes and recent haircuts." This is why Brian isn't too worried about his mother being alone in the big house where he grew up.

The street is still, despite his mother's suspicions, an old-fashioned neighbourhood, with women who watch out windows recording events, daytimes, to share with each other over the phone, evenings. Brian still smarts a bit at this network, although it's been sixteen years since it conveyed to his parents the news that he, at fourteen, had been spotted downtown, smoking. This intelligence made it home before Brian himself and imagining the neighbours' involvement —their culpability—made him feel doubly punished, victimized.

Growing up, Brian hated anyone to have power over him. He despised even how his sister, Carole, eighteen months older, could make his life miserable in petty, absolute ways —"I'll tell Mom. Mom!"—and he dreamt of being an only child. Now Carole is living in Vermont with a not-divorced man (which may or may not have killed their father, depending on their mother's magnanimity when she brings this up) and Brian feels the weight of being his mother's only accessible child. She needs him, and Brian resents being obligated. He sees his childhood as something like a compulsory cocktail party. Now that a decent interval has passed, his attendance has been noted, it's time to find the hostess, shake hands and say goodbye, perhaps arranging a lunch date for some time in the middle future.

He takes another drag of his cigarette and realizes he's exhaling carefully, away from the receiver, so his mother won't hear him. When Beaver hands him the drink, he takes a deep pull, miming excessive need for Beaver's benefit. Beaver only shrugs and moves over to start a deliberately casual inspection of the bookshelves. Beaver's real name is Michael Hinther, a secret almost as well-kept as his real age, which is 26. Brian knows this because he found Beaver's driving-licence when he was looking through his wallet for a laundry ticket. But if Beaver wants to be, forever, nineteen, that's fine with Brian. People should be able to create themselves as best they can, to his mind; any other reality is just another version of original sin. The trick of it is, of course, that the self-creation has to be absolutely seamless.

He thinks his mother would worry less if she got out of the house more. She's still an active woman, or could be, 60-something isn't old anymore, and he considers square-dancing groups, bus tours to historic sites, elaborate picnics with huge smoked hams, whole roast chickens. And white linen tablecloths, that's a nice touch. He doesn't suggest these things to his mother; she has a perverse streak that might surface. He can imagine her, spitefully, joining a singles brunch group instead, tinting her hair to a colour like apricot or champagne, and becoming one of those brittle, preserved women with their talk of eye-lifts, isometrics, diets and men with American Express Gold Cards. Brian sees these women at some of the places he goes to—places with names like Dinkies and Little Eden and Wallbanger City—and suffers for their exposure of tooth and nail, their trying to hold on. He thinks his mind is not large enough to contain the concept of "mother" in tandem with "bikini waxing."

"The silver would get top price from a fence these days." There is something casually satisfied in his mother's voice, as if the theft has already occurred and, with much grace, she is not saying "I told you so."

"No, no, I took that to the bank." Brian sits up, alarmed. Beaver turns from the bookshelves, a large paperback of David Hockney prints open in his hands. "You didn't bring that back to the house, did you?"

"Not the good silver," she says quickly. "The second best."

"Oh, the plate." Brian sits back, relieved. Since turning 30, he's developed a sense of personal responsibility to the concept of history, a desire, perhaps, to have his place and time in the world marked, accounted for. Although he finds no room in his own life for clutter and ritual—his future is not clear enough to him for the commitment that would suggest: what does he want to be when he grows up?—he feels this is possible because his past is kept elsewhere, all in a piece. He can always start over.

"On Saturday, when you're here," his mother goes on.

"I'm coming Saturday?"

"For dinner. And I want you to look over this brochure I got from the cable company. They have some kind of alarm system for the house. I can't make out how it works. Do you suppose it hooks up to the television?"

"I'll have a look at it.

"My mother," he announces to Beaver, unnecessarily, after hanging up.

"I thought we were going out Saturday."

"We never go out before ten. I can do both."

"You mean, you can fit me in?"

"Getting a little close in here, isn't it?" Brian carries his drink across the room. From the window he can see all the way down Century Street, right to the centre of town. On some still nights in the early spring and fall, if he has the windows open and the stereo off, he can hear the bells of the city hall clock. He doesn't open the window in the summer —from June to September he rents an air-conditioner— because nine floors below, along one side of the parking-lot, are all the garbage bins from his building and the Cantonese restaurant next door. In July, however, he can see the fireworks exploding silently in the black sky framed by the window, more real than they would be if he was out in the evening, distracted by the sounds of children up past their bedtimes, solicitous parents, hawkers and vendors, even the crackle and boom of the fireworks themselves. This makes up for not hearing the bells in the summer, when they might make him nostalgic for the sounds he used to hear carried over the lake at his parents' summer place. He would lie in his dark room, listening, and wonder how many hours had passed since he was sent to bed, how many hours until morning. It's been a while since his assumption was, naturally, that tomorrow would be a day better than today.

Brian turns the knob to Low Cool and opens the exhaust. The created breeze sends six or seven dust bunnies scurrying across the bare floor, to hide under the couch.

"Did I ever tell you how tidy I am?" Beaver asks. "I even do windows. A rare thing, let me tell you."

"Don't start," Brian warns. He recently read an editorial that suggested the phrase "postal service" was oxymoronic. He laughed and tried to think of his own. The only thing that came to mind was "healthy relationship."

"Or you'll make me leave before the piggies?" Beaver asks, grinning. But he adds, "Do you want me here or not?" with the inflection of a real, not rhetorical question.

What Brian wants is not to have the choice. When he started high school he was given a list of elective subjects and told to fit two into his timetable. The typing he wrestled with as if it were a difficult, foreign language. "J" he would translate, "right hand, first finger, home row." Only by staying after school, the tock-tock of the old Underwood hollow and forlorn in the empty room, was he able to pass the course, with a dismal eleven-words-a-minute in a class that averaged thirty-four. The Latin, actually being a foreign language, went somewhat better, although it remains isolated in his mind, a singular pocket of clauses and cases too explicit to apply to anything else. Since, he has been suspicious of that gift—choice—and looks for the deprivation in abundance, the catch.

"*Exigeant sum,*" he says. He puts his drink down on the willow blanket hamper he uses as a coffee table and stretches his hands in front of him, fingers laced, knuckles cracking. "Old bones. Can we talk about something else?"

"Of course," Beaver says, disingenuous. "So." He sits on

the arm of the couch, his feet hooked around the leg so he can lean back with his spine straight, six inches clear of the cushions. "How is your mother?"

"She thinks someone is watching her house."

"Really, where does she live?"

"I never told you?" Brian names the suburb, shaking his head. "I can't think of a safer place. Practically her whole life is there. My whole life is there."

"I can understand that," Beaver says, sitting up properly and crossing his legs, ankle over knee. One of his socks has snared a dust bunny and his foot looks haloed, diffuse. "It would be easy enough to think of time past as something taken away, and want to hold onto other things. Ageing as a kind of violation. I do not have that kind of trauma, myself, you understand. Not yet. I'll save that one for my own sunset years." He tilts his head to one side, framing his face with his hands, palms out. "I'll think about it tomorrow," he says.

"Beaver," Brian says. "That's very near profound, what you said."

"I am only shallow," Beaver says, with great dignity, "on the surface. I know as much about insecurity as the next guy. It's about losing control."

From the open book on the coffee table, Hockney's portrait of his own parents faces up. Brian slumps back, against the window frame. Is there a Latin word for *window?* Beaver gets up and stands close beside him. He smells warm and cottony, like fresh ironing. Brian puts his arm around him, across the small of his back, and holds him, idly considering what anyone who looked up through the window would see. Both men are roughly the same height, over five-ten but under six feet, with the medium-dark colouring Beaver calls "low Episcopal." Brian hopes their attraction suggests, for each of them, a healthy self-image.

He lightly rests his chin on Beaver's shoulder, looking

down. Mrs. Hockney sits in a plain trestle-chair, her hands clasped in her lap, staring intently forward. Off to her left, Mr. Hockney is in profile, bent from the waist to examine closely a large book held open in his lap. Mr. and Mrs. Hockney.

"So, you want me to stay?" Beaver asks in a quiet voice. "Or do we just have this warm moment?"

"Tonight," Brian says. "I want you to stay tonight."

Brian teaches high-school science. Tries to teach, rather; the marking is not going well. "What is the coloured part of the eye?" he asked on the exam. "Cones," fully one-third of the class responded. A bonus question, "How many eyes does a bat have?" had been read as a trick, and most of the students answered, "None."

What is going on here? he wonders. When he was their age he was experimenting with drugs, but he doesn't see any signs of that in his classes. The kids' eyes are clear and untroubled, evidently only their minds are unfocused. How is he supposed to reach them, to make them thrill to verifiable principles? He wants to shake them up, to yell, "You little bastards, this kind of inattention is just selfishness!" But his chance has passed, he is supposed to hand in the low-pass grades and wait until September for another.

He pushes the unmarked papers into a file folder, checks to make sure he has his wallet and keys, glances at his watch. He's due at his mother's at five, then to meet Beaver at Little Eden at ten. It's 2:30.

The hardware store is in an underground mall below a chain hotel. Brian parks on a metered side street and enters the hotel lobby, where there is a bank of elevators. A man is waiting there, and he nods as Brian stands beside him, hands held behind his back. "Hello." The man's voice is deep, with a slight rhythmic inflection. A Norwegian accent, something like that. He has the pale looks of the actor who played Jackal in that movie. Brian thought he was attractive, although Beaver's opinion was that the actor's teeth looked like a snow fence in March.

"Hello," Brian says. The elevator arrives and Brian steps back to let the man enter first. He presses 12; Brian, M-1. There is a long delay after the doors slide closed. Brian pushes the button marked Close Door, to encourage the mechanism. He looks at the other man and makes a faintly apologetic shrug. He doesn't want to appear impatient, but he doesn't want to be defeated by a machine, either.

"Are you in the hotel?"

"No, I live in town," Brian says, then looks at the elevator panel, the conflicting instructions: up and down. "I wasn't thinking."

The man appears to give this careful consideration. He nods. The elevator shudders and starts up.

"I am the winner, then."

"I guess you are," Brian agrees.

On the twelfth floor the man steps out, then turns back. "Coming?" he asks, and Brian steps out of the elevator. Following him down the hall, Brian watches the centre seam of the man's jacket, where the pattern meets in a solid colour like the no-passing line on a highway. He hears the elevator slide closed and the car, unoccupied, moving down.

The hotel room has a double bed, an upholstered chair, a combination desk and dresser, colour television bolted to a wall shelf and a rollaway cot, open and made.

"What's this?" Brian asks, pointing. "Are you expecting someone?"

"Don't talk, please," the man says, shrugging out of his jacket. "Say nothing."

Brian, silent, raises his hand to unbutton his shirt cuff. This is, after all, the other man's fantasy.

Syphillis, he thinks. Gonorrhea. Jesus, herpes. But panic stays back, guilt refuses to land. His afternoon was a minor corruption, no worse, really, than the parking-ticket he has stuffed into the glove compartment. Already, this is in the past, a closed chapter. He swings wide, turning. The car's muffler scrapes on the slope of the driveway, and the rough sound brings Brian's mother to the front door. She calls out as he slides the shift into Park. He can't make out her words, her voice competing with a lawnmower somewhere in the neighbourhood. He lets himself out of the car and stands in the wedge between the open door and the car's body.

"Right on time," she says, stepping quickly along the sidewalk. She is wearing a skirt and blouse, flat-heeled shoes and looks, Brian thinks, to be about 40. Where, in the face of this evidence, does he get his ideas of what ages look like? Maybe from Beaver. He can imagine, while he's sleeping, a slow osmosis of values, the pores of his skin open and receptive. His mother makes quick, patting touches on his forearm. They're not the type to hug. "You look all bright-eyed and healthy," she says. "Have you been jogging?"

"You know me better than that," Brian says. "I guess it's just clean living."

"Even as a child you were healthy. Both my children were, although your sister had that awful skin in her teens. Remember? Pizza-on-toast you called it."

"A sensitive child," Brian mumbles.

"I wonder if that man knows what she looked like? He must have seen photographs, surely. Maybe I should send some, for Christmas."

"Meow," Brian says. "Sensitivity must run in the family." He waves across the street and is rewarded by a twitching of Mrs. Chiccini's drapes. "You're being watched," he tells his mother, and she shakes her head, clucking. Brian slides one of the cardboard boxes from the back seat of the car and lays it at her feet. "I stopped at the hardware store and got you these."

She bends and pulls one of the screens from the box. As she holds it up to the sky, her face is dappled with the light that passes through the grill, shapes like the clubs in a deck of cards.

"It's very heavy," she says. "Pretty, though. What's it for?"

"They're for the basement windows," Brian says, lifting the other box from the back seat. "I'll show you."

In the basement, as he works, Brian develops an easy, competent rhythm: screws sink themselves in flush security; crumbling mouldings form themselves into right angles under his hands; he feels masculine and charismatic. Above him, the house has the not-unpleasant weight of an adult decision. After he's done four of the six windows, his mother appears at his elbow, surprising him. He'd forgotten she lives here.

"You look so intense," she says. "Men at work."

Brian wipes his hand across his forehead. The gesture is for his mother; even in summer the basement is cool, and the work is not difficult. "I'd like to finish today."

"I could bring your dinner down here," she says. "We could set up the card table, like a little picnic indoors. It's chicken."

Brian remembers the card table. One winter when school was closed by an outbreak of strep throat he and Carole, spared, had played endless games of Go Fish. "Mom!" he remembers his sister's voice. "Mom, Brian says he doesn't have any eights and I saw one in his hand." "Why are you looking at your brother's cards?" asked their mother from the top of the stairs. "I am trying," Carole said, smug and wise, "to keep him honest."

"Come here, I want to show you how these work." He slides one of the windows open. He's installed the metal screens between the two panes of glass. "You see, you can still open them, for air, but nothing else. And you can't remove them from outside, only from down here."

"I see," his mother nods. "Aren't you clever? Your father was never good with his hands. Not that I minded, but it seems a man should be able to do things around the house, not call a repairman for every fuse and fan belt." She shakes her head. "The money that goes on repair, just maintenance things, ordinary wear and tear. It's history now, but when I think of the days I sat around waiting for the plumber or the furnace man." She makes a tetch-sound with her front teeth.

"A house is a big responsibility," Brian agrees. "But it has its rewards, your own place."

She slides the window closed, then back open, and doesn't comment. "What about if there's a fire?"

"Leave the building in an orderly fashion." It's what Beaver would say, an automatic response no longer requiring thought. "I don't know," he admits. "I didn't think about getting out. Maybe you just better not start any fires down here."

"I'm sorry. I didn't mean to slight your work. But my concern isn't only for real estate."

"Weren't you going to get me some dinner?" Brian asks.

"Oh," his mother says, slipping into the tone of voice most familiar to Brian. "You never liked any kind of disagreement."

"That's right." Brian turns away from her, back to work.

When she brings down the tray of fried chicken, green and yellow wax beans, roast potatoes, Brian is surprised to see an opened bottle of beer, half-poured with a neat head into one of the cut-glass water tumblers. The only times he drinks at his mother's are when he brings wine for dinner, at Thanksgiving and Christmas.

"Did you get this for me?"

She looks flustered, and smooths her hands over her skirt

several times, her eyes glancing from the furnace to the stationary tubs, avoiding Brian.

"What?" Brian grins, unable to imagine what's caused this reaction. "Did I say something?"

"It's not that." She looks at him levelly, with some effort. "I got the beer for Mr. Daly." There is a proud note in her voice, an enviable possessiveness.

"Daly? From 143?" Brian steps over to the window, tiptoes up to look at the direction of that house number. "Him?"

"I just happened to mention that the washer was giving me some trouble. The spin cycle? And he offered to look at it. Well, I didn't think I could offer him coffee or tea in the middle of the afternoon, a grown man."

"No, I guess you couldn't." Brian raises the glass and takes a sip of beer, toasting his new status. "And the washing-machine?" he asks.

"Oh, it's fine," she says quickly. Then. "You're teasing me."

"Just a little," Brian admits. But to keep the joke contained, before it can become a part of the family, he waggles a chicken leg at her with a cautioning gesture. "There are some things a son doesn't have to know, okay?" She looks up at him, inhaling with a short gasp, and Brian steps back, suddenly serious. "When I finish these windows," he says. "Do you understand? Once I finish these windows, nobody will be able to get in here. Nobody."

Trying to keep a safe distance between himself and a black Trans-Am, Brian misses his turn and has to circle the block to get into the parking-lot behind Little Eden. It's a few minutes past ten, but still he takes his time locking the steering-column, rolling up the window, snapping off the radio so it won't crackle and blare when he starts the car later. He knows he has been told, in a loopy, oblique way, that his mother will be needing him less. Instead of feeling unburdened, as he should, he feels that he has been accused of something, the sense he has when the phone rings and rings, then stops just as he picks up the receiver. A connection has been missed.

Inside, Little Eden is over-cooled, pleasant for Brian, who has driven with the car window open and feels his skin filmed with dust and exhaust, although he knows he will be clammy in a few minutes. He stands still, adjusting to the patterned light from Tiffany lamps, the music pumping into the room, then spots Beaver sitting with a very pregnant woman in one of the banquettes. Weaselling through the crush of bodies radiating from the centre bar, he steels himself to meet one of Beaver's "young ladies." Women attach themselves to Beaver, oblivious to his disinterest, constructing their own myths about a gentleman "not like the others." His sympathy for these women and their expectations is diluted by the pain they cause Beaver, his wide-eyed bewilderment, "What did she want?" Brian can only shrug; it isn't in him to explain Beaver's charm, to answer what it is that might have been wanted. It may be desire, rather than "sensibility" that Beaver mocks when he lists, "Ralph Lauren sweaters, a fridge full of Perrier and all the latest Broadway show albums. Welcome to the not-quite-real world." Brian, unable to voice *Not me?*, settles for a Brando mumble, responding, "The banal. The banal."

"I'm a little late," he says, sliding into the banquette beside Beaver.

"That's okay," Beaver says. "I ordered for you."

"Jesus, Beaver." Brian has just noticed the drink at his place, a half-pineapple, scooped out and filled with a viscous yellow fluid. This is topped with not one but two paper parasols. He has to laugh. "What is it?"

"No-one knows. The bartender just invented it. Margot made a few suggestions."

"Margot." Brian nods to acknowledge the introduction. He takes a tentative sip and winces, his back teeth registering an instant protest. He waves to stop a passing waitress and orders another round for the table, substituting a scotch for the pineapple. "Thanks for trying," he says to Beaver.

"Are you finished with this?" the waitress asks, putting one hand on the pineapple.

"Yes, I'm the scotch," Brian says.

"After this, scotch?" she asks, putting the paper parasols on the table in front of Brian. "You get to keep them."

"Well, thank you," Brian says. Under the table, Beaver's thigh is warm against his own. Across the table, Margot is lining up her empty glasses for the waitress to clear away.

"Scotch, after your nice drink?" Beaver asks when the waitress is gone. "Don't you know, never mix never worry?"

"I guess my mother never told me that one. Is that what you learned at your mother's knee?"

"At my mother's knee I learned only what a boney knee looks like," Beaver says quickly. It's obviously something he's said before. Then he looks down into his drink. "Actually, the only things I remember her specifically telling me were, Always iron silk in one direction and, Never sleep with your face on a handbag. I think she wanted a daughter."

"Really?" Brian starts to laugh, but controls himself. It's possible Beaver has shared with him something important and revealing. He's never mentioned his mother before; he usually presents himself as having been created, complete, at nineteen. "Listen," he says, keeping his voice light. "In an era of erroneous zones and being your own best friend, those are probably not bad rules to live by."

"They're so important, rules to live by," Margot says. She pushes her hair back from her forehead and Brian, who knows a story introduction when he hears one, composes the muscles of his face to look pleasant, interested. "I had wanted," she says, "to have a perfect driving record—no demerits—and absolute fidelity in my marriage." She had managed both, she tells them, until the afternoon her brakes failed and she zipped through a red light into the back of a parked police cruiser. After that, she blazed a trail of promiscuity that ended with a messy divorce and a painful pelvic inflammation. Telling this to Brian and Beaver, her face takes on the swollen, pouched look of a woman about to cry, and Brian tactfully suggests she might not want to finish her Comfort Stinger. "Oh, drinking can't hurt me," she says. "I even drank castor oil. Have you ever? It's like trying to swallow vaseline, you practically have to chew it." She looks down at her tummy, shaking her head sadly. "I'm just going to be preggy forever."

Alarmed, Brian leaves some bills on the table and hustles Beaver out of Little Eden and into the car.

"Hey, don't let the breeders get you down," Beaver says, then stops talking while Brian gentles the accelerator, trying to get the engine to turn over.

"The only thing worse than a machine is a machine that doesn't work," Brian grumbles. Then, as his effort is rewarded, "Don't say 'breeders.'"

"Yes, sir," Beaver says. "I didn't know it bothered you."

"Well, it does." Brian speeds up, to catch a green light before it changes. It doesn't bother him, not really. "And I'm starting to feel a little guilty about leaving like that. Maybe you could tell her I'm manic-depressive or something?"

"Honesty's the best policy?" Beaver slides closer to Brian. The car seat dips and creases with a moist, puckering sound. "I've never seen her before in my life. She said we could share the table."

"Is that true?" Brian glances over at Beaver, side-lit by the passing streetlights. "And she told you something that personal?"

"Who else would she tell? You wouldn't want to try that on your friends. They might change their opinion of you. Why risk it?" Beaver shrugs, an arcing, helpless motion Brian can feel through the car's seat.

They are silent. Brian, who has never in his life considered confiding in a stranger, is remembering the Norwegian's sudden talkativeness, after. He had thought the story was necessary to the man's idea of intimacy, a belief that he was not casual, had more than the one dimension. Perhaps that was the point of the fantasy; the silent, non-judgmental audience. He sees his building up ahead, the blocks of light on the sheer brick side facing Century, and has a vision of one person behind each window, lips moving silently, comforted by the words themselves, as if they had no meaning, were incantations or prayers so explicit they could not be translated into experience.

"Look at them," Beaver says, as the car's headlights sweep the parking-lot. There are three teenaged boys leaning on the hood of a car. They are all wearing jeans and black T-shirts with large, glittering decals on the fronts—Black Sabbath, Led Zeppelin, Grateful Dead—groups Brian has known and forgotten.

"Yeah, I see them," he says. He used to call this "hanging out" but his students say "hacking around."

"Ten years ago I would have been one of them," Beaver says. "Now I'm afraid of them. Even the Beaver doesn't get to be nineteen forever."

"Oh, Beaver." This admission is so close to what Brian was thinking, was feeling, he doesn't turn the car to back into his space, but leaves the engine idling as he opens his door. He has his back to Beaver when he says, "Take the car. Go back to your place and get what you need, then come back. Okay?"

"What?"

"Toothbrush. Clean underwear. I don't know." Brian's

shrug restates Beaver's earlier one: why risk it?

"Why don't you come with me?" Beaver asks, but he's sliding across the seat, taking his place behind the wheel.

"I don't want to do any choosing," Brian admits. "You do that. I'll be up there."

"What if I come back with a coffee table or a television or something?"

"Then we'll live with a coffee table," Brian says. He swings the car door closed, and stands to one side. Beaver backs out of the lot, tooting the horn before he eases onto Century.

Alone in his apartment, Brian considers having a quick shower, or at least changing his clothes. He is uncertain what he would want this to mean. It could be penance, or an alibi. The apartment is small and warm and he moves to turn on the air-conditioner.

He stands at the window, looking down to where his car should be. The parking-lot is like a wide smile, with a tooth missing. Once, watching out this same window, he had seen a road crew repair a pothole beside a storm grating. When they were done, one of the three men had opened the grating and, using a rake to extend his reach, had pulled from the sewer a travel bag, similar in size and shape to those sold by airlines. This one, however, was a solid burgundy colour and even from nine storeys up looked expensive. The other two workers had moved in, blocking Brian's view, as the first held the bag open for their inspection. Then the bag was tossed onto the back of the open truck, where Brian could see it as the workers drove away. It sat on a neat pile of two-by-fours, visible until the truck turned off Century.

Why does he think of that now? It's less than half a story; he never learned any more than he had seen. Brian presses his forehead to the window. The breeze from the air-conditioner is cool on his neck. The vibration through the glass tickles his ear. He hates not knowing how things turn out, whether or not a story has a happy ending.

Victims of Gravity

On his first Sunday as a married man, Nick wakes slowly. "It's as if they were never pierced at all," the woman had said, stroking her earlobe. "I just stopped wearing the earrings." They were on a subway, rattling through blocks of light and dark. Nick had struggled to see her face, but she turned away from him, exposing only the line of her neck. While his dream shreds and recedes to its soft world of symbols and solutions he lets himself drift into consciousness.

With his eyes still closed, he takes inventory; his arms here, legs there, his head sunk deep in the pillow. He can feel the cat sleeping against his side, solid as a ham. "I'm okay," he tells himself. "I'm going to be okay," he amends.

"Good morning," he calls out, hearing Linda in the kitchen, the sound of running water. This sound is so mundane, so clear with everyday purpose, he feels it must be a response to his own resolution; he is going to be okay. He flips himself out of bed, sending the cat from the room at a fast trot, landing squarely on his feet.

Over breakfast, Nick decides to re-enter his life slowly, taking one thing at a time.

"I'm going up to the school, for softball," he tells Linda. "Want to come and root for me?"

"You must be joking. I don't have time for anything like that. There are a million things for me to do before we go to my folks." She is wearing an old pair of corduroy slacks, worn bald at the seat and inside the thighs, with one of Nick's shirts half-buttoned over these. Nick thinks she looks boyish and sloppy, and absolutely charming.

"That's tonight?" Nick asks, remembering the invitation, but vaguely, as if it had been given to someone else; someone else must have responded. "We just saw them last week." He carries his plate to the sink and stands there, looking out the window. "Couldn't we make it some other time?"

"Listen, when you get back," Linda says, "could you leave your shoes outside? I want to do something with these floors."

"My shoes?" Nick steps back from the sink and looks down at his Nikes. Under them, the floor looks as it always has, small grey and blue squares spreading out in concentric circles, orbiting farther and farther away from him. He realizes he's holding his breath and exhales carefully, so he won't sigh. He is being cautious and formal, a married person. The cat crosses in front of him, weightless with feline purpose. "The cat comes in on little fog feet," Nick says, thinking Eric would have liked that. Nick likes it; it feels like his first appropriate response to his environment in weeks.

"What?" Linda's eyes are opaque with disinterest.

"Never mind." Nick turns his back. "You're sure you don't want to come with me?"

"I'm sure." Linda comes up beside him, nudging him out of the way so she can reach the tap to rinse out her coffee mug. "You have fun."

By the time Nick finishes getting ready, Linda is on the phone, confirming the time for dinner with her mother. Nick remembers his own mother, sitting in the kitchen to talk on the black, wall-mounted telephone. She wore, always, a two-piece wool suit; her legs—one almost completely coiled around the other when she was perched on the edge of the chrome dinette chair—were encased in shiny nylon stockings of an orange sheen he has not seen since. On a Sunday, the table in front of her would support her hat and gloves. He waves as he passes the kitchen, his hand raised to his temple like a salute, then stops when he hears her call out to him.

"Yes?" He stands still. The doorknob is smooth and egg-shaped in his hand.

"You won't forget, about your shoes?"

"I won't forget." Nick lets the door close behind him and steps into the clear morning, the sounds of the city coming to him all at once, as if they had been waiting for his appearance. He walks down Century, on the sunny side of the street, to the corner of Elm, before crossing to the school campus.

On Sundays, before, Nick played softball with Eric on the back campus of the high school where they both taught. Some of the seniors joined them, enough to make two short teams. Eric, who handled his history classes with a firm authority, was subjected to extensive razzing about his pitching, which was slow and loose.

"Drill it man, burn it home," the guys yelled at him. "Don't make it so easy."

Eric laughed out loud and pitched the way he always did, in a predictable straight line over the plate. Then, turning to watch the struck ball, he had an amazed expression, as if no-one had ever connected with one of his pitches before. In Special Ed. class at college, when they were learning American Sign Language, nobody had to look at Eric's hands to figure out what he was trying to say. Everything was written on his face.

"It wasn't so easy," he said, sheepish, when Nick and he and his girlfriend Peg went for pizza and beer. "It had a little dance to it."

"Dance, hell. It was a funeral. Hey, what's a good dance for a funeral, Peg?" Nick wanted to include her in the conversation, or to have her feel included. He wasn't sure what level of familiarity was expected of him. His first year at the school, Peg was on maternity leave, so he knows more about her than he's heard from her, more than he's heard, even, from Eric. He knows she's a year older than he, that she was a professional dancer, jazz or modern, for a few years before marrying and taking the job in the school office, and that she had a baby boy. Mark? Matthew? Michael? No, Matthew is right. "A gavotte?"

"Too formal," Peg shook her head, brushing a few crumbs from her cheek. "A tarantella, the way you guys play, all formless and frenzied until you drop."

"Tarantella. Tarantula," Eric said, splaying the fingers of one hand rigidly on the tabletop, pushing them down from the wrist, then lifting up. "Push-ups on a mirror."

"No, that's this one." Peg put the fingers of both hands together, flexing them against each other. "I should know. It's about Matt's level."

"How is Matt?" Nick asked. Once, when he was playing outfield, he glanced over the campus to his left and saw her, Peg, sitting on the hood of Eric's car, combing her hair in the morning light, before the sun was directly overhead. That, along with the sophistication he imagined because she was divorced with a four-year-old son, warmed him with an easy, transparent want.

"He's great." Peg raised one hand and deliberately brought it, fisted, into the space between her breasts. "My heart is full," she said solemnly, without a trace of self-consciousness. Eric snorted and Nick was saved from embarrassment by recognizing the line from a movie.

"Saint Peg," Eric intoned, causing Nick to choke on his beer. "Saint Peg the Miracle-less."

"Oh, stop it," Peg said, and Eric assumed a posture of contrition, lowering his head and feigning great fascination with the menu before him. "How's, Linda?" she asked Nick, barely pausing before the name.

"Fine, I guess." Nick heard the hesitation in her question, before the name. He wished, for a moment, he could confide in her something true and revealing, or at least make the kind of comment that a woman would find interesting. Say, "She finds working on her doctorate is teaching her a lot about herself," or, "She's decided social work is an option before she locks herself into any choices." He really doesn't know what those comments would mean. "She doesn't go out much," he says. "I don't know."

"Yes," Peg nodded, as if she understood this.

"This place used to have lentil burgers." Eric looked up, a lock of hair diagonally over his forehead giving him a surprised appearance. "I don't see them here."

"I guess no-one returned them," Peg offered.

"What?"

"The burgers, I guess no-one returned them," Peg started. Then, "Lentil! You said, Lentil. I thought you said, Rental burgers."

"Me, too," Nick agreed. "I was trying to figure out how it worked, but I couldn't get my mind any further than that they'd come with a paper tablecloth."

"You're both mad." Eric sat back, crossing his arms in his shiny green bowling-jacket, an authentic relic discovered at the Crippled Civilians, with "Fraser" heavily cross-stitched over the left shoulder.

Nick reached out and pulled some melted cheese from the plate of pizza, perfectly content.

"Come on, Eric. Give me some help with this."

That Friday Eric was killed when his car spun out of control over a patch of road being resurfaced on the outskirts of town. The accident was not connected to events in the lives of Eric and Nick. It was pointless, fatal. Nick was 28; disturbing doubts about God were in his past and in his future; he was convinced, only, of his own solitude.

When Linda suggested he should not be alone after the funeral, Nick agreed. He agreed to everything; choice was not in him. He had, in fact, no concept of what his agreement would entail. Time had ceased to be continuous to him. Anything might happen. Certainly he would still be alone, with his past amputated from him he was singular and incomplete. Less than five weeks later, with no sense of cause-and-effect, he found himself walking through a formal church wedding. There were 68 guests at the reception afterwards, mostly Linda's family and their friends, all strangers to Nick. He couldn't tell you now if it had rained that day, or was sunny and clear. Later, in the photographs, he will notice that he has the first two fingers of his right hand held oblique across the palm of his left. The sign for What. *What?*

"Hey, Mr. Thornton," one of the guys calls to Nick as he lets himself through the chain-link fence. "Long time no see."

"Yeah, I'm back." Nick recognizes the boy, Bob Markham, from his class. He can't remember seeing him standing before, although he knows he's played softball almost weekly. "What team am I on?" He stands behind the plate and picks up one of the bats, swinging it experimentally, with an exaggerated, critical concentration.

"We sort of had the teams already set up," Bob says, looking down at the ground.

"Time stands still for no man, is that it?" Nick says. He makes a noise, a meaningless snort or chuckle, trying to reassure the boy that this distance isn't necessary, but this is artificial and painful to Nick.

"Well." Bob looks at him, eyes slightly narrowed. "You could be in the field."

"Sure." Nick nods. Then he looks, closely, at the boy in front of him. There is a patch, just where Bob's cheek angles down to his jaw, which has been missed in the last shave. The fine hairs there, too soft to be called stubble, grow all in one direction, as ordered and distinct as the petals of a flower. They are separated by no more than ten or eleven years, Nick thinks, and he takes a step forward. "What are you planning to do after school?" he asks.

"On Sunday? Oh, I see. Well, college."

"No, after that, even."

"I don't know." Bob looks uncomfortable. "Like, get a job or something. You know, reality."

"Reality," Nick repeats. The word is hard-edged in his mouth, like a cracked cough drop. He waves one hand in the air in front of him, unable to articulate a question, the dismissive gesture the same as the one he uses in class when the period ends. "Don't mind me."

"I don't, Mr. Thornton," Bob says. "You know, we're all real sorry about your friend. Mr. Heinz, he was okay." Bob stands in front of Nick as if he's about to say more, then he shrugs and puts his hands into his pockets as if they were too heavy for his arms to support.

"Yeah," Nick agrees. "He was okay." He turns and starts toward the outfield. At the back of the campus he raises his arm and shouts, "Let's get this show on the road." Then he sees Eric at the side of the campus—knowing in the same moment it's Peg, wearing Eric's bowling-jacket—and he yells, "Hey! Hey!"

By the second "hey" he is walking quickly toward her. She stands on the sidewalk on the other side of the fence, not watching his approach, and Nick is afraid she will bolt, start running away from him. Comic-book heroes fill his mind as he considers ways to stop her: a long, flexible arm like Elastic Man; a speed-of-light sprint like the Flash; an entangling web shot from his wrist like Spiderman. Lacking these resources, he feels clumsy and inadequate. This is similar to the feeling he had as a child, when he would wake from a dream of flight and find himself, still, a victim of gravity.

"Peg." Nick puts one hand up, his fingers curled through the fence, and leans toward her, imprisoned behind the diamonds of wire mesh. "I'm glad I saw you. What are you doing here?"

"I'm in the neighbourhood, Sundays," she says, keeping

her profile to him. "Matt's reading group is just up there. I hang around."

"Yeah? I haven't seen you." This sounds like an accusation. "I haven't been here, myself." They begin walking together, Peg on the sidewalk and Nick on grass splotched with white lime powder, with the fence between them.

"Matt reads?" Nick asks, after a silence. He's imagined the reading group to be a kind of Great Books Society, intent in a discussion of *Pat the Bunny*.

"No, he's read to," Peg says. "Sometimes I forget he's a kid, you know? He's a friend."

Nick pauses, searching. Then, "What do you tell a friend, about what happened?"

"I never lied to him about life ending badly. I used to tell him he wouldn't have to worry for a long, long time. I thought his interest was personal. I never thought of anything like this." She brushes a strand of hair from her mouth, where a light breeze has lifted it. "I guess he won't believe me anymore. Maybe he'll never ask me what makes the sky blue, and I've already done my homework on that one. You're supposed to work at having them trust you, kids. All the time."

They come to the end of the fence, where the gate is, and Nick lets himself through to stand with her on the sidewalk.

"What now?" he asks.

They start walking up Elm, stopping together at the curb for a moment, although there's no light. They step into the street again at the same moment, as if they've been signalled to do this.

"Does Matt trust you?" Nick starts, after Peg has been quiet, walking with her head down, her hands in the pocket of the green jacket.

"I guess he does. I'm not sure what the point is. I trusted his father—like, I felt I was supposed to—and I might have been better off not to, right from the beginning. Or maybe I shouldn't have thought it was so important. You know, lower my expectations. Not make demands. Never nag." She laughs, a short, unamused sound. "I've said those things before, can't you tell?"

Nick scuffs the suede toe of his Nike along the sidewalk, instead of answering. Peg stops, looking down at the shoe, then points. "Your lace."

He kneels in front of her to re-tie his track shoe, feeling a smooth mastery of the situation as he twists the lace into a perfect bow, taking time to make the ends even. "There." He stands up.

"You do that just like Matt. All rigid concentration and perfection. I wonder what it means, about his personality? How's yours, are you a well-adjusted person?"

"No," Nick says, being honest after some deliberation. "No, I don't think that I am."

"Sorry." Peg looks down at her own feet, lining up the ends of her shoes with a crack in the sidewalk. "I shouldn't have asked."

"I didn't have to answer. I wanted to."

"Don't do that," Peg says, her voice sharp.

"Do what?"

"Act like there's something between us. We don't have anything more in common than we did six weeks ago. We don't even really know each other, okay?"

"No." Nick leaves the single syllable uninflected.

"You know what's supposed to happen now, don't you? I'm supposed to take this off." Peg runs one hand over the bowling-jacket, under the gold collar where it meets the green body. "And tell you that Eric would have wanted you to have it. Maybe he would have, but I'm not giving it to you. I love having this jacket all to myself. I'm even living in his apartment, did you know that? It was just about the only thing his family wasn't crazy to consider an asset." She looks up at Nick, her hair wild and careless over her face.

She beats at it, to push it back with a blunt, closed fist. Nick steps forward automatically, raising his hand to stop her. "No," she says, leaning away from him. "I'm not going to cry. I'm being," she stops to rub her nose with the sleeve of her jacket, "brave. I don't have anything to share with you."

"I guess not," Nick agrees.

"I have to pick up my kid. Don't come with me, okay?" She turns, walking away quickly, bent over. Nick has not asked her where Eric was going to, or coming from, that night; he understands that he is never to know. The past is closed off. He stands on the sidewalk, imagining he can hear the softball game still in progress, way back there, going on without him.

"The honeymoon couple!"

He hears Ian Grant's voice boom through the door. The sound seems to displace the air in the long hall before the door is pulled open and his father-in-law stands in front of Nick and Linda.

"Well," Ian says. "Well, well."

"Three holes in the ground?" Nick offers, at the same time extending his hand for a hearty pumping.

"Hi, Daddy." Linda steps past Nick and into the living-room. She raises her arms, hands lightly closed and limp at the wrists, presenting herself for a hug.

"Hi, Lindy."

"Is that them?" Betsy Grant's voice pierces the wall between the living-room and the kitchen. "I'll be right in."

"Go give your mother a hug," Ian says, pushing Linda away. "We'll be out here. Come on, Nick."

Nick follows the older man across the room, idly wiping his palm on the pocket flap of his jacket. He notes the difference between this room and his own living-room. Here, the carpet is thick and plush, the furniture heavily upholstered. Nick lives with bare floors and pine knockdowns from a

Scandinavian shop.

"Now, what can I get you to drink?"

"Scotch, I guess," Nick says, moving closer to the liquor cabinet. Linda and her mother come out of the kitchen, close and talking quietly.

"Oh, that's good for us," Betsy says, raising her voice. She comes up to Nick and lays one hand on his arm. "We're having veal," she tells him, imparting this message as a confidence.

"You know," Nick carries a drink, diluted to the colour of winter sunlight, across the room to Linda. "I used to think that veal came from a separate animal. Like chicken from chickens, lamb from lambs."

"Ham from pigs, beef from cows." Linda shakes her head. "It doesn't hold up, that thinking."

"Well, wait, it gets worse." Nick picks up his glass and takes half the scotch in one swallow. "When someone told me it comes from calves, I thought they meant these." He almost tips the remains of his drink as he taps the muscle below the back of his knee. "I had only learned how to spell it—calves—and I was baffled by the connection." He looks around the room, at Betsy nursing her own drink, Ian staring past him to some other reality outside the window, Linda twisting a strand of hair around her fingers. After a silence, Nick asks, "Am I talking funny or something? I didn't expect a big laugh, but—"

"It's a nice story," Betsy interrupts. "We can take our drinks to the table."

Nick sits at his place, across the table from Linda, and eats in silence while she talks to her family about how much work she's doing to turn Nick's apartment into a "home."

"Really, Mummy, he keeps his socks and underwear in a toy box. Like that."

"Oh, men," Betsy agrees, shaking her head.

Nick imagines if he looks up Ian will give him a conspiratorial wink. He feels his temples pounding and closes his eyes, leaning forward. He opens his eyes and looks down in his lap. The white napkin there suddenly blossoms with a red, red rose. He stares, perplexed, until another spot spreads itself over the soft cloth.

"Oh my god." He pushes his chair back from the table. "My nose is bleeding. Excuse me." He leaves the room with the napkin pressed against the bridge of his nose, trying to remember what he learned about this condition in Boy Scouts: how much pressure is therapeutic? He hears the table fall silent behind him, just for a moment, then all three voices speak at once.

In the bathroom, Nick soaks the napkin and holds it against his nose, splashing cold water on his face with his other hand. After what seems a very long time the bleeding slows, then stops, the water running down the drain tinged with pink, then clear. He wrings the napkin nearly dry, pats his face with it, then spreads it over the edge of the sink. With a heavy sigh, he lowers the toilet-seat cover and sits down, stretching his legs out in front of him, his boots pressed against the side of the bathtub.

There is a short, soft knock on the door.

"Nick?" Linda asks, pushing the door open and stepping into the room. "You okay?" She leans back against the door, pushing it closed.

"I guess." Nick glances sideways at her, but remains seated. "I'm not making a very good impression."

"I told them it was probably the scotch."

"Oh, great. Thanks a lot. Now they think I can't handle liquor."

"No, it's not like that at all. What's the matter with you?"

"You know what I heard in the staff lounge? Remember that television show, *Wild Kingdom,* where they'd go after a different animal each week? One of the teachers was saying that the whole thing was a fake. Like when the narrator would say," Nick lowers his voice, aiming for a broadcasting tone, "'On our way to observe the mating dance of the snowy egret, we spotted this fellow in a bit of a jam.' And there'd be a woolly marmot or something—a furry little mammal, always—stuck in a tree. The crew would stop and rescue it with all this equipment they had with them. 'After giving the little fellow a helping hand, we were back on the egret trail.' Do you remember that?"

"I remember those shows. So what?" Linda turns to stand in front of the sink, the counter at the level where her blouse tucks into her skirt, avoiding the damp napkin.

"Brian, this other teacher, was saying that they were all faked. That woolly marmot was put in the tree by the crew in the first place. Even the egrets were from the San Diego Zoo or some place." Nick shakes his head slowly. "It was all a big fake."

"Is there a point to this?" Linda leans forward, closer to her reflection. She combs her fingers through her hair, flipping the ends over her shoulders. Then she rubs at one corner of her mouth with her ring finger, frowning. She props one hip against the sink and turns back to Nick. "What are you trying to tell me?"

"Don't you feel betrayed by that? Like, there's absolutely nothing left to count on in the world. I'd always reassured myself that no matter what happened to us," he waves his hand in a sweeping arc to include all of humanity. "In all the aridity and disenchantment," now he raises his hand, loosely fisted, "the wild kingdom was still unfolding according to plan. It was still a beautiful world." He falls silent, rubbing one hand back and forth over the toilet-paper holder. The unrolled paper jerks up and down like an elevator trying to level itself.

"Wait." Linda crosses her arms over her chest. "I want to

be sure I understand this. You are upset, to the point of a nosebleed, because *Wild Kingdom* was faked. Maybe faked. Have I got that right? Is there anything else?"

Nick brushes at the knees of his slacks, then leans forward, putting his elbows on his thighs and cupping his chin in his hands. How can he tell her he needs her to sit on the hood of his car, combing her hair in the clear light of morning while he plays games to win her, again and again? How can he tell her that the game is what he is playing for, rather than the outcome? How can he tell her the condition of his kitchen floor gives him no clues to the inevitability of his own survival?

"I think," he says slowly. "This isn't going to work out. Us."

"What? What are you talking about?" Linda pulls back from the sink, standing unsupported in the middle of the bathroom. "I'm willing to work at this relationship."

"Relationship? Well, yes, sure." He lets his voice trail off, unable to say anything for a while. "You're right. We could work at this, the relationship, and sort of polite each other to death, staying together. But that's not what I want." He looks up at her.

"Go ahead, then. Tell me," Linda commands, raising her hands to her neck, closing her fingers into knots against the soft skin there.

"No." Nick shakes his head. He curls his toes inside his boots, to take up less space, a fetal position of the feet. His insteps press against leather, the smooth hide of some animal.

"You started this."

"Okay." Nick takes a breath and fixes his gaze into the middle distance. "This is not going to work and I want out."

"Don't say that." Linda lowers her voice as she speaks. "I can't believe you said that to me in a bathroom. Why did you marry me at all?"

"You didn't want me to be alone." Nick shrugs, to discount the cost of admitting this; it's vaguely impolite, self-serving, to remind one of a favour performed.

"Alone? Alone? What about me?"

"You've got them." Nick tips his head at the bathroom door.

"Don't you say a word to them. Leave them out of this. We are going back out there and you are not going to say anything about this. I'm not discussing this in here."

Nick stands and turns, bending to lift the toilet-seat. "I'll be out in a bit." He pulls down his fly. "Do you mind?"

"Remember," Linda cautions, letting herself out of the room and pulling the door closed after her.

When she's gone, Nick does up his fly, puts the cover back down on the toilet and sits with his body twisted at the waist so he can rest his forehead on the cool sink. His life, to this moment, arranges itself behind him. In front of him, the marbled counter is blurred and indistinct. He is too close to focus properly.

When his mother died, he had been judged too young to attend the burial; he was allowed in the church, but not to the grave. One of his mother's friends had taken him to her car, where she had tilted the rear-view mirror so she could reapply her lipstick, talking to him all the while around that pink cylinder. Later, they went to a restaurant ("I know you boys are always hungry," she said) and this woman, nameless to him, chain-smoked. Nick's mother never smoked in public; this woman never stopped. Hearing the word "funeral" when it spread deafeningly through the teachers' lounge, Nick had not thought of his friend, not thought of Eric at all. His mind had been filled with this woman, exhaling smoke through her nose while biting into a toasted club-sandwich.

He raises his head and looks around, as if he expects to see that someone has come in and joined him. He stands quietly and goes over to the door, turning the knob slowly and pulling it open silently. He steps out, listening intently, then walks down the hall away from the living-room.

The master bedroom door is open, and Nick steps into the room walking on tiptoe, with an unnecessary stealth. He can hear Linda and her parents laughing, the clink of glass and a scraping sound, a knife against china.

There is, as Nick had hoped there would be, a telephone in the darkened room, on the night table at the right side of the queen-sized bed. Nick remains standing, rather than crease the bedspread, and picks up the receiver, holding it to his ear until he hears the dial tone. Then, pleased to be able to do this by memory, he dials Eric's number. Before the first ring, during the confused jangle of far-off, electronic noises, he tips his head toward the door, satisfied he can still hear Linda talking to her parents.

"Hello?" The voice that answers, on the fourth ring, is still young enough to inflect those two syllables with hope.

"Hello, Matt?" Nick speaks quickly, his voice just barely above a whisper. "Is your mother home?"

"Mom!" Matt has obviously turned from the phone without covering the mouthpiece, calling to his mother. Nick crouches down with the effort of listening through the distance that separates them. "Mom, it's for you. A man with a deep voice."

With the first two fingers of his right hand, Nick depresses the buttons on the telephone, cutting off the connection. He will explain this to Peg later, if he sees her again. With his left hand still clutching the receiver, he brings it close to his chest, sinking back to sit on the bed. The feeling that pulses through his body elevates his spirit so that he barely wrinkles the bedspread beneath him. This racing surge, this clear emotion, will be called redemption. He has made contact.

Rohinton Mistry

Condolence Visit

Yesterday had been the tenth day, *dusmoo,* after the funeral of Minocher Mirza. *Dusmoo* prayers were prayed at the fire-temple, and the widow Mirza awaited with apprehension the visitors who would troop into her house over the next few weeks. They would come to offer their condolences, share her grief, poke and pry into her life and Minocher's with a thousand questions. And to gratify them with answers she would have to relive the anguish of the most trying days of her life.

The more tactful ones would wait for the first month, *maasiso,* to elapse before besieging her with sympathy and comfort. But not the early birds, they would come flocking from today. It was open season, and Minocher Mirza had been well known in the Parsee community of Bombay.

After a long and troubled illness, Minocher had suddenly eased into a condition resembling a state of convalescence. Minocher and Daulat had both quietly understood that it was only a spurious convalescence, there would be no real recovery. All the same, they were thankful his days and nights passed in relative comfort. Minocher had been able to wait for death freed from the agony that had racked his body for the past several months. And as it so often happens in such cases, along with relief from physical torment, the doubts and fears that had tortured his mind released their hold as well. He was at peace with his being that was soon to be snuffed out. Daulat, too, felt at peace because her one fervent prayer was being answered. Minocher would be allowed to die with dignity, without being reduced to something less than human; she would not have to witness any more of his suffering.

Thus Minocher had passed away in his sleep after six days spent in an inexplicable state of grace and tranquillity. Daulat had cried for the briefest period; she felt it would be sinful to show anything but gladness when he had been so fortunate in his final days.

Now, however, the inevitable condolence visits would make her regurgitate months of endless pain, nights spent sleeplessly, while she listened for his breath, his groans, his vocalization of the agony within. For bearers of condolences and sympathies she would have to answer questions about the illness, about doctors and hospitals, about nurses and medicines. She would be requested, tenderly but tenaciously, as if it was their entitlement to recreate the hell her beloved Minocher had suffered, instead of being allowed to hold on to the memory of those final, blessed six days. The worst of it would be the repetition of details for different visitors at different hours on different days, until that intensely emotional time she had been through with Minocher would be reduced to a dry and dull lesson learned from a textbook, which she would parrot like a schoolgirl.

Last year, Daulat's nephew, Sarosh, the Canadian immigrant who now answered to the name of Sid, had arrived from Montreal for a visit. He had brought her a portable cassette recorder, remembering her fondness for music, so she could tape her favourite songs from All-India-Radio's two Western music programs: "Merry Go Round" and "Saturday Date." But Daulat had refused it, saying: "I listen to music, and poor Minocher sick in bed? Never." She would not change her mind despite Sarosh-Sid's recounting of the problems he had had getting it through Bombay Customs.

Now she wished she had accepted the gift. It could be handy, she thought with bitterness, to tape the details, to squeeze all of her and Minocher's suffering inside the plastic case, and proffer it to the visitors who came propelled by custom and convention. When they held out their right hands in the condolence-handshake position (fingertips of left hand tragically supporting right elbow, as if the right arm, overcome with grief, could not make it on its own) she could thrust toward them the cassette and recorder: "You have come to ask about my life, my suffering, my sorrow? Here, take and listen. Listen on the machine, everything is there on tape. How my Minocher fell sick, where it started to pain, how much it hurt, what doctor said, what specialist said, what happened in hospital. This button? Is for Rewind. Some part you like, you can hear it again, hear it ten times if you want: how nurse gave wrong medicine but luckily my Minocher, sharp even in sickness, noticed different colour pills and told her to check; how wardboy always handled the bedpan savagely and shoved it underneath as if he was doing sick people a big favour; how Minocher was afraid when time came for sponge bath because they were so careless and rough—it felt like number three sandpaper on his bedsores, my brave Minocher would joke. What? This FF button? Means Fast Forward. If some part bores you, just press FF and tape will turn to something else: like how in hospital Minocher's bedsores became so terrible it would bring tears to my eyes to look, all filled with pus and a bad smell on him all the time, even after sponge bath, so that I begged of doctor to let me take him home; how at home I changed his dressing four times a day using sulfa ointment, and in two weeks bedsores were almost gone; how, as time went by and he got worse, his friends stopped coming when he needed them most, friends like you, now listening to this tape. Huh? This letter P stands for Pause. Press it if you want to shut off machine and ask more details of your friend Minocher's suffering...."

Daulat stopped herself. Ah, the bitter thoughts of a tired old woman. But of what use? It was better not to think of these visits which were as inevitable as Minocher's death. The only way out was to lock up the flat and live elsewhere for the next few weeks. Perhaps at a boarding-house in Udwada, town of the most sacrosanct of all fire-temples. But though her choice of place would be irreproachable, the timing of her trip would generate the most virulent gossip and criticisms the community was capable of, to weather which she possessed neither the strength nor the audacity. The visits would have to be suffered, just as Minocher had suffered his sickness, with forbearance.

The doorbell startled Daulat. This early in the morning could not bring a condolence visitor. The clock was about to strike nine as she went to the door.

Her neighbour Najamai glided in, as fluidly as the smell of slightly rancid fat that always trailed her. Today it was supplemented by curry *masala,* Daulat realized, as the odours found and penetrated her nostrils. It was usually possible to tell what Najamai had been cooking; she carried a bit of her kitchen with her wherever she went.

Although about the same age as Daulat, widowhood had descended much earlier upon Najamai, turning her into an authority on the subject of religious-rituals-and-the-widowed-woman. This had never bothered Daulat before. But the death of Minocher offered Najamai unlimited scope and she had made the best of it, besetting and bombarding Daulat with advice on topics ranging from items she should pack in her valise for the four-day Towers of Silence vigil, to the recommended diet during the first ten days of mourning. Suddenly Najamai had metamorphosed into an unbearable nuisance. But her counselling service had to close shop with completion of the death rituals, and Daulat was again able to regard her in the old way, with a mixture of tolerance and mild dislike.

"Forgive me for ringing your bell so early in the morning but I wanted to let you know, if you need chairs or glasses, just ask me."

"Thanks, but no-one will come—"

"No, no, you see, yesterday was *dusmoo,* I am counting carefully. How quickly ten days have gone! People will start visiting from today, believe me. Poor Minocher, so popular, he had so many friends, they will all visit—"

"Yes, they will," said Daulat, interrupting what threatened to turn into an early morning prologue to a condolence visit.

Najamai, meanwhile, had spied Minocher's pugree.

"Oh, that's so nice, so shiny and black, in such good condition!" she rhapsodized.

It really was an elegant piece of headgear, and many years ago Minocher had purchased a glass display case for it. Daulat had brought it out into the living-room this morning.

Najamai continued: "You know, pugrees are so hard to find these days, this one would bring a lot of money. But you must never sell it, never. It is your Minocher's, so always keep it." With these exhortatory words, she prepared to leave. Her eyes wandered around the flat for a last-minute scrutiny, the sort that evoked mild dislike for her in Daulat.

"You must be very busy today, so I'll—" Najamai turned toward Minocher's bedroom and halted in mid-sentence, in consternation: "*O baap ré!* The lamp is still burning! Beside Minocher's bed—that's wrong, very wrong!"

"I forgot all about it," lied Daulat, feigning dismay. "I was so busy. Thanks for reminding. I'll put it out."

But she had no such intention. When Minocher had breathed his last, the family priest had been summoned, and he gave her careful instructions on what was expected of her. The first and most important thing, the *dastoorji* had said, was to light a small oil lamp at the head of Minocher's bed; this lamp, he said, must burn for four days and nights, no more and no less, while prayers were performed at the Towers of Silence. But the little oil lamp became a source of comfort in a house grown quiet and empty for the lack of one silent feeble man, one shadow. She kept the lamp lit past the prescribed four days, replenishing it constantly with coconut oil.

"Didn't *dastoorji* tell you?" asked Najamai. "For the first four days the soul comes to visit here. The lamp is there to welcome the soul. But after four days, prayers are all complete, you know, and the soul must now quickly-quickly go to the next world. If the lamp is still burning the soul will be attracted to two different places—here, and the next world. You must put it out, you are confusing the soul," Najamai earnestly concluded.

Nothing can confuse my Minocher, thought Daulat, he will go where he has to go. Aloud she said, "I'll put it out right away."

"Good, good," said Najamai, "and oh, I almost forgot to tell you, I have lots of cold-drink bottles, Limca and Goldspot, if you need them."

What does she think, I'm giving a party the day after *dusmoo?* thought Daulat. In the bedroom she poured more oil in the glass, determined to keep the lamp lit as long as she felt the need. Only, the bedroom door must stay closed, so the tug-of-war between two worlds, with Minocher's soul in the middle, would not provide sport for visitors.

She sat in the armchair next to what had been Minocher's bed and watched the steady, unflickering flame of the oil-lamp. Like Minocher, she thought, reliable and always there; how lucky I was to have such a husband. No bad habits, did not drink, did not go to the racecourse, did not give me any trouble. Ah, but he made up for it when he fell sick. How much worry he caused me then, while he still had the strength to argue and fight back. Would not eat his food, would not take his medicine, would not let me help with anything.

In the lamp glass coconut oil, because it was of the unrefined type, rested golden-hued on water, a natant disc. With a pure, sootless flame the wick floated, a little raft upon the gold. And Daulat, looking for answers to difficult questions, stared at the flame. Slowly, across the months, borne upon the flame-raft, came the incident of the Ostermilk tin. It came without the anger and frustration she had known then. It came in a new light. And she could not help smiling as she remembered.

It had been the day of the monthly inspection for bedbugs. Due to the critical nature of this task, Daulat tackled it with a zeal unreserved for anything else. She worked side by side with the servant. Minocher had been made comfortable on the armchair and the mattress was turned over. The servant removed the slats, one by one, while Daulat, armed with a torch, examined every crack and corner. Then she was ready to spray the mixture of Flit and Tik-20, and pulled at the handle of the pump. But before plunging it in to poison every potential redoubt of *cimex lectularius,* she glimpsed, between the bedpost and the wall, a large tin of Ostermilk on the floor. The servant dived under to retrieve it. The tin was shut tight, she had to pry the lid open with a spoon. And as it came off, there rose a stench powerful enough to rip to shreds the hardy nostrils of a latrine-basket collector. She quickly replaced the lid, fanning the air vigorously with her hand. Minocher seemed to be dozing off, olfactory nerves unaffected. Was he trying to subdue a smile? The tin without its lid was placed outside the back door, in hopes that the smell would clear in a while.

The bedbug inspection was resumed and the Flitting finished without further interruption. Minocher's bed was soon ready, and he fell asleep in it.

The smell of the Ostermilk tin had now lost its potency. Daulat squinted at the contents: a greyish mass of liquids and solids, no recognizable shapes or forms among them. With a stick she explored the gloppy, sloppy mess. Familiar objects began to emerge gradually, greatly transmogrified but retaining enough of their original state to agitate her. She was now able to discern a square of fried egg, exhume a piece of toast, fish up an orange pip. So! This is what he did with his food! How could he get better if he did not eat. Indignation drove her back to his bedroom. She refused to be responsible for him if he was going to behave in this way. Sickness or no sickness, I will have to tell him straight.

But Minocher was fast asleep, snoring gently. Like a child, she thought, and her anger had melted away. She did not have the heart to waken him; he had spent all night tossing and turning. Let him sleep. But from now on I will have to watch him carefully at mealtimes.

Talking to visitors of such things would not be difficult. But they would be made uncomfortable, not knowing whether to laugh or keep the condolence-visit-grimness upon their faces. The Ostermilk tin would have to remain their secret, hers and Minocher's. As would the oxtail soup, whose turn it now was to come sailing silently out of the past, on the golden-discus flame-raft of Minocher's lamp.

At the meat market Daulat and Minocher had always argued about oxtail, which neither had ever eaten. Minocher wanted to try it, but she would say with a little shudder, "See how they hang like snakes. How can you even think of eating that? It will bring bad luck, I won't cook it."

He called her superstitious. But oxtail remained a dream deferred for Minocher. After his illness began, Daulat shopped alone, and at the butcher's she would remember Minocher's penchant for trying new things. She was often tempted to buy oxtail and surprise him—something different might revive his now almost-dead appetite. But the thought of bad luck associated with all things serpentine dissuaded her each time. Finally, when Minocher had entered the period of his pseudo-convalescence, he awakened on the second day after a peaceful night and said, "Do me a favour?" Daulat nodded, and he smiled wickedly. "Make oxtail soup." And that day, they lunched on what had made her cringe for years, the first hearty meal for both since the illness had commenced.

Daulat rose from the armchair. It was time now to carry out the idea she had had yesterday, walking past the Old-Age Home for Parsee Men on her way back from the fire-temple. If Minocher could, he would want her to give away his clothes, as he had often done. Many were the times he had gone through his wardrobe selecting things he did not need or wear anymore, wrapped them in brown paper and string, and carried them to the Home for distribution.

Beginning with the ordinary items of everyday wear, she started to sort his clothes: *sudras,* underwear, two spare *kustees,* sleeping suits, light cotton shirts for wearing around the house. She decided to make parcels right away—why wait for the prescribed year or six months or even a month and deny the need of the old men at the Home if she could (and Minocher certainly could) give today?

When the first heap of clothing took its place upon brown paper spread out on his bed, something wrenched inside her. The way it had wrenched when he had been pronounced dead by the doctor. Then it passed, as it had passed before. She concentrated on the clothes; one of each in every parcel —*sudra,* underpants, sleeping suit, shirt—would make it easier to distribute.

Bent over the bed, she worked unaware of her shadow on the wall, cast by the soft light of the oil-lamp. Though the curtainless window was open, the room was half-dark because the sun was on the other side of the flat. But half-dark was light enough in this room into which had been concentrated her entire universe for the duration of Minocher's and her ordeal. Every little detail in this room she knew intimately: the slivered edge of the first compartment of the chest of drawers where a *sudra* could snag, she knew to avoid; the little trick, to ease out the shirt-drawer that always stuck, she was familiar with; the special way to jiggle the key in the lock of the Godrej steel cupboard she had mastered a long time ago.

The Godrej cupboard Daulat tackled next. This was the difficult one, containing the "going-out" clothes: suits, ties, silk shirts, fashionable bush shirts, including some foreign ones given by her Canadian nephew, Sarosh-Sid, and the envy of Minocher's friends. This cupboard would be the hard one to empty out, with each garment holding memories of parties and New Year's Eve dances, weddings and *navjotes*. Strung out on the hangers and spread out on the shelves were the chronicles of their life together, beginning with the Parsee formal dress Minocher had worn on the day of their wedding: silk *dugli,* white silk shirt and the magnificent pugree in its glass case in the living-room.

She went to it now and opened the case. The pugree gleamed the way it had 40 years ago. How grand he had looked then, with it splendidly seated on his head! There was only one other occasion when he had worn it since, on the wedding of Sarosh-Sid, who had been like a son to them. Sarosh's papers had arrived from the Canadian High Commission in New Delhi, and three months after the wedding he had emigrated with his brand new wife. Minocher had wanted Sarosh to wear the pugree but he, however, had insisted like so many modern young men on an English-styled double-breasted suit. So Minocher had worn it instead. Pugree-making had become a lost art due to young men like Sarosh, but Minocher had known how to take care of his. Hence its mint condition.

Daulat took the pugree into the next room and looked for the advertisement she had clipped out of the *Jame-Jamshed.* It had appeared six days ago, on the morning after she had returned from the Towers of Silence: "Wanted—a pugree in good condition. Phone no. ——." Yesterday Daulat had called the number, the advertiser was still looking. He was coming today to inspect Minocher's pugree.

The doorbell rang. It was again Najamai from next door. In her wake followed her servant, Ramchandra, lugging four chairs of the stackable type. Her rancid-fat-curry-*masala* smell was embroidered by the attar of Ramchandra's hair oil, and the combination made Daulat wince.

"Forgive me for disturbing you again, I was just now leaving with Ramchandra, many-many things to do today. And there is no-one at home if you need chairs so I brought them now only. That way you will...."

Daulat had stopped listening. Good thing the bedroom door was shut, or Najamai would have started another oil-lamp exegesis. Would this garrulous busybody never leave her alone? There were chairs in the dining-room that could be brought out.

With Sarosh-Sid's cassette recorder, she could have made a tape for Najamai too. It would be a simple one to make with many pauses during which Najamai did all the talking: Neighbour Najamai Take One—"Hullo, come in (long pause)...hmm...right (short pause)...yes yes...that's okay (long pause)...hmm...right (short pause)...yes yes...that's okay (long pause)...right, right...." It would be no trouble, compared to the tape for condolence visitors.

"...you are listening, no? So chairs you can keep as long as you like, don't worry, Ramchandra can bring them back after a month, two months, after friends and relatives stop coming. Come on, Ramu, come, we're getting late."

Daulat shut the door and withdrew into her flat. Into the silence of the flat where moments of life past and forgotten, moments lost, misplaced, hidden away, were waiting to be recovered. They were like the stubs of cinema tickets she came across in Minocher's trouser pockets or jacket, wrung through the laundry, crumpled and worn thin, but still decipherable. Or like the old program for a concert at Scot's Kirk by the Max Mueller Society of Bombay, found in a purse fallen, like Scot's Kirk, into desuetude. On the evening of the concert, Minocher, with a touch of sarcasm, had quipped: Indian audience listens to Germans perform German music inside a church built by skirted men from Scotland—truly Bombay is a cosmopolitan city. The encore had been *Für Elise.* The music passed through her mind now in the silent flat: the beginning in A minor, full of sadness and nostalgia and yearning for times gone by; then the modulation into C major, with its offer of hope and understanding. This music was like a person remembering—if you could hear the sound of the workings of memory, *Für Elise* is what it would sound like.

Remembering suddenly seemed extremely important, like some deep-seated need surfacing, manifesting itself in Daulat's flat. All her life those closest to her had reminisced about events from their lives; she, the audience, had listened, sometimes rapt, sometimes impatient. Grandmother would sit her down and tell stories from years gone by; the favourite one was about her marriage and the elaborate matchmaking that preceded it. Mother would talk about her Girl Guide days, with a faraway look in her eyes; she still had her dark blue Girl Guide satchel, frayed and faded.

When grandmother had died no music was allowed in the house for three months. Even the neighbours had silenced their radios and gramophones for ten days. Daulat's brothers were forbidden to play cricket in the compound outside the building for a month, and they had taken it very hard. After sulking around the house for a while they tried to interest themselves in reading, the only activity that seemed suitable enough for a house in mourning. A few days passed and the two were captivated by the world of books, which was probably the best thing grandmother had done for her grandsons. During this time, Daulat's mother introduced her to kitchen and cooking—there was now room for one more in that part of the flat. With the exception of oxtail soup, Daulat had learned the various dishes which a man would desire. Grandmother's death taught the brothers to feed minds and the sister to feed bellies. And when Minocher's belly, on his deathbed, craved oxtail soup, she quickly learned that dish as well.

Daulat had become strangers with her radio shortly after Minocher's illness had started. But the childhood proscription against music racked her with guilt whenever a strand of melody strayed into her room from the outside world. Minocher's favourite song was "At the Balalaika." During their courtship he had taken her to see *Balalaika,* starring Nelson Eddy, at a morning show. It was playing at the Eros Cinema, and Minocher had been surprised that she'd never seen it before. It was his fourth time. How did the song...? She hummed it, out of tune: "At the Balalaika, one summer night a table laid for two, was just a private heaven made for two...."

The wick of the oil lamp crackled. It did this when the oil was low. She fetched the bottle and filled up the glass, shaking out the last drop, then placed the bottle on the windowsill: a reminder to replenish the oil.

Outside, the peripatetic vendors had started to arrive. The potato-and-onion man got louder as he approached: "Onions rupee a kilo, potatoes two rupees," faded as he went past, to the creaking obligato of his thirsty-for-lubrication cart. He was followed by the fishwalli, the eggman, the biscuitwalla, and the ragman who sang with a sonorous vibrato:

Of old saris and old clothes I am collector
Of new plates and bowls in exchange I am giver....

From time to time, BEST buses thundered past and all sounds were drowned out. Finally came the one Daulat was waiting for. She waved the empty bottle at the oilwalla, purchased a quarter litre, and arranged with him to knock at her door every alternate day. She was not yet sure when she would be ready to let the lamp go out.

The clock showed half past four as she went in with the bottle. Minocher's clothes lay in neat brown paper packages, ready for the Old-Age Home. She shut the doors of her cupboards now almost empty, and thought, the clothes it takes a man a lifetime to wear and enjoy can be parcelled away in hours.

The man would soon arrive to see Minocher's pugree. She wondered what it was that had made him go to the trouble of advertising. Perhaps she should never have telephoned. Unless he had a good reason she was not going to part with it. Definitely not if he was just a collector.

The doorbell. Must be him, she thought, and looked through the peep-hole.

But standing outside were second cousin Moti and her two grandsons. Moti had not been at the funeral. Daulat did not open the door immediately. She could hear her admonishing the two little boys: "Now you better behave properly or I will not take you anywhere ever again. And if she gives you Goldspot or Vimto or something, be polite and leave some in the glass. Don't drink it all unless you want a pasting when you get home."

Daulat had heard enough. She opened the door and Moti, laden with eau-de-cologne, fell on her neck with woeful utterances and tragic tones. "Oh Daulat, Daulat! What an unfortunate thing to happen to you! Oh very wrong thing has come to pass! Poor Minocher gone! Forgive me for not coming to the funeral, but Peshotan's gout was so painful that day. Completely impossible. I said to Peshotan, least I can do now is visit you as soon as possible after *dusmoo*."

Daulat nodded, tried to look grateful for the sympathy Moti was so desperate to offer. It was almost time to reach for her imaginary cassette player.

"Before you start thinking what a stupid woman I am to bring two little boys to a condolence visit, I must tell you there was no-one at home they could stay with. And we never leave them alone. It is so dangerous. You heard about that vegetablewalla in Pherozeshah Baag? Broke into a flat, strangled a child, stole everything. Cleaned it out completely. *Parvar Daegar!* Save us from such wicked madmen!"

Daulat led the way into the living-room, and Moti sat on the sofa. The two boys occupied Najamai's chairs. The bedroom door was open just a crack, revealing the oil-lamp with its steady unwavering flame. Daulat shut it quickly lest Moti should notice and comment about the unorthodoxy of her source of comfort.

"Did he suffer much before the end? I heard from Rati—you know Rati, sister of Eruch Uncle's son-in-law Shapoor—she was at the funeral, she told me poor Minocher was in great pain the last few days."

Daulat reached in her mind for the start switch of the cassette player. But Moti continued: "Couldn't the doctors do something to help? From what we hear these days, they can do almost anything."

"Well," said Daulat, "our doctor was very helpful, but it was a hopeless case, he told me."

"You know, I was reading in *Indian Express* last week that doctors in China were able to make"—here, Moti lowered her voice in case the grandsons were listening, shielded her mouth with one hand, and pointed to her lap with the other—"a man's Part. His girlfriend ran off with another man and he was very upset. So he chopped off"—in a whisper—"his own Part, in frustration, and flushed it down the toilet. Later he regretted it in hospital, and God knows how, but the doctors made for him"—in a whisper again—"a New Part, out of his own skin and all. They say it works and everything. Isn't that amazing?"

"Yes, very interesting," said Daulat, relieved that Moti had, at least temporarily, forsaken the prescribed condolence visit questioning.

The doorbell again. Must be the young man for the pugree this time.

But in stepped ever-solicitous Najamai. "Sorry, sorry. Very sorry, didn't know you had company. Just wanted to let you know I was back. In case you need anything." Then leaning closer conspiratorially, rancid-fat-curry-*masala* odours overwhelming Daulat, she whispered, "Good thing, no, I brought the extra chairs."

Daulat calculated quickly. If Najamai stayed, Moti would drift even further from the purpose of her visit. Najamai would also be pleased. So she invited her to sit. "Come in, please, meet my second cousin Moti. And these are her grandsons. Moti was just now telling me a very interesting case about doctors in China who made"—copying Moti's whisper—"a New Part for a man."

"A new part? But that's nothing new. They do it here also now, putting artificial arms-legs and little things inside heart to make blood pump properly."

"No no," said Moti. "Not a new part. This was"—in a whisper, dramatically pointing again to her lap for Najamai's benefit—"a New Part. And he can do everything with it. It works. Chinese doctors made it."

"Oh!" said Najamai, understanding everying. " A New Part!"

Daulat left the two women and went to the kitchen to open a bottle of Goldspot for the children. The kettle was ready and she poured three cups of tea. While she arranged the tray, the doorbell rang, for the third time. This had to be the young man. She was ready to abandon the tray and go to the door but Najamai called out, "It's all right, I'll open it, don't worry. Finish what you are doing."

Najamai said "Yes?" to the young man standing outside the door.

"Are you Mrs. Mirza?"

"No no, but come in. Daulat! There's a young man here

asking for you."

Daulat settled the tray on the teapoy before the sofa and went to the door. "You're here to see the pugree. Please come in and sit." He took one of Najamai's chairs.

Najamai and Moti exchanged glances. Come for the pugree? What was going on?

The young man felt obliged to say something. "Mrs. Mirza is selling Mr. Mirza's pugree to me. You see, my fiancée and I, we decided to do everything the proper traditional way at our wedding. In correct Parsee dress and all."

Daulat heard him explain in the next room and felt relieved. It was going to be all right, parting with the pugree would not be difficult. The young man's reasons would have made Minocher exceedingly happy.

But Najamai and Moti were aghast. Minocher's pugree being sold and the man barely digested by vultures at the Towers of Silence! Najamai decided to take charge. She took a deep breath, tilted her chin pugnaciously. "Look here, *bawa,* it's very nice to see you want to do it the proper way. So many young men are doing it in suits and ties these days. Why, one wedding I went to, the boy was wearing a shiny black suit with lacy, frilly-frilly shirt and bow tie. Exactly like Dhobitalao Goan wedding of a Catholic it was looking! So we are happy about you." She paused, took another deep breath, and prepared for a fortissimo finale. "But this woman who is giving you the pugree, her husband's funeral was only ten days ago! Yesterday was *dusmoo.* And today you are taking away his pugree! It is not correct! Come back later!" With that, Najamai went after Daulat, and Moti followed.

The young man could see them go into a huddle from where he was and could hear them as well. Moti was saying, "Your neighbour is right, this is not proper. Wait for a few days."

And Najamai was emboldened to the point of presenting

one of her theories. "You see, with help of prayer the soul crosses after four days. But sometimes the soul is very attached to this world and takes longer to make the crossing. And as long as the soul is here, everything like clothes, cup-saucer, brush-comb, all must be kept same way it was, exactly same. Or the soul becomes very unhappy."

The young man was feeling uncomfortable. He, of course, had not known that Daulat had been widowed as recently as ten days ago. Once again he felt obliged to say something. "Excuse me, maybe I should come back later for the pugree, the wedding is three months away."

"Yes! Yes!" said Najamai and Moti together; Najamai continued: "I don't want you thinking I'm stirring my ladle in your pot, but that would be much better. Come back next month, after *maasiso*. You can try it on today, see if it fits. In that there is no harm. Just don't take it away from the place where the soul expects it to be."

"I don't want to give any trouble," said the young man. "It's all right, I can try it later. I'm sure it will fit."

Daulat, with the pugree in her hands, approached the young man. "If you think it is bad luck to wear a recently dead man's pugree, and you are changing your mind, that is okay with me. But let me tell you, my Minocher would be happy to give it to you if he were here. He would rejoice to see someone get married in his pugree. So if you want it, take it today."

The young man looked at Moti and Najamai's flabbergasted countenances, then at Daulat waiting calmly for his decision. The tableau of four persisted: two women slack-jawed with disbelief; another holding a handsome black pugree, and in the middle an embarrassed young man pulled two ways, like Minocher's soul, in a tug-of-war between two worlds.

The young man broke the spell. He reached out for the pugree and gently took it from Daulat's hands.

"Come," she smiled, and led him into the bedroom, to the dressing-table. He placed the pugree on his head and looked in the mirror.

"See, it fits perfectly," said Daulat.

"Yes," he answered, "it does fit perfectly." He took it off, caressed it for a moment, then hesitantly asked, "How much...?"

Daulat held up her hand. She had prepared for this moment; though she had dismissed very quickly the thought of selling it, she had considered asking for its return after the wedding. Now, however, she shook her head and took the pugree from the young man. Carefully, she placed it in the case and handed it back to him.

"It is yours, wear it in good health."

"Thank you," said the young man. "Thank you very much." He waited for a moment, then softly, shyly added, "And God bless you."

Daulat smiled. "If you have a son, maybe he will wear it too, on his wedding." The young man smiled back.

She saw him to the door and returned to the living-room. Moti and Najamai were sipping half-heartedly at their tea, looking somewhat injured. The children had finished their cold-drink. They were swishing the shrunken ice cubes around in the forbidden final quarter-inch of liquid, left in their glasses as they'd been warned to, to attest to their good breeding. An irretrievably mixed-up and confusing bit of testimony.

A beggar was crying outside. "Firstfloorwalla *bai!* Take pity on the poor! Secondfloorwalla *bai!* Help the hungry!"

Presently, Najamai rose. "Have to leave now, Ramchandra must be ready with dinner." Moti took the opportunity to depart as well. "After a severe gout attack Peshotan hates to be left for too long."

Daulat was alone once more. Leaving the cups and glasses where they stood with their dregs of tea and Goldspot, she went into Minocher's room. It was dark except for the glow of the oil-lamp. The oil was again low and she reached for the bottle, then changed her mind.

From under one of the cups in the living-room she retrieved a saucer and returned to his room. For a moment she stood before the lamp, looking at the flame. Then she slid the saucer over it, covering up the glass, the way his face had been covered by a white sheet ten days ago.

In a few seconds the lamp was doused, snuffed out. The afterglow of the wick persisted; then it, too, was gone. The room was in full darkness.

Daulat sat in the armchair. The first round, at least, was definitely hers.

Lend Me Your Light

...your lights are all lit—then where do you go with your lamp? My house is all dark and lonesome, lend me your light.—Rabindranath Tagore, *Gitanjali*

We both left Bombay the same year. He first, for New York, then I, for Toronto. As immigrants in North America, our sharing of this common experience should have salvaged something from our acquaintanceship. It went back such a long way, to our school days.

To sustain an acquaintance does not take very much. A friendship, that's another thing. Strange, then, that it has ended so completely, and I will probably never meet him again.

Jamshed was my brother's friend. The three of us went to the same school. Jamshed and my brother Percy, both four years older than I, were in the same class, and spent their time together. They had to part company during lunch, though, because Jamshed did not eat where Percy and I did, in the school's drillhall-cum-lunchroom.

To this drillhall were delivered lunches from homes all over the city. The tiffin carriers would stagger into the school compound with their long, narrow, rickety crates balanced on their heads, each with 50 tiffin boxes. When the boxes were unpacked, the drillhall would be filled with a smell that is hard to forget, thick as swill, as the individual aromas of 400 steaming lunches started to mingle. The smell must have soaked into the very walls and ceiling. No matter what the hour of the day, that hot and dank grotto of a drillhall smelled stale and sickly, the way a vomit-splashed room does even after the vomit is cleaned up.

Jamshed did not eat in this crammed and cavernous interior. Not for him the air redolent of vomit-lunch odours. His food arrived precisely at one o'clock in the chauffeur-driven air-conditioned family car, and was eaten in the leather-upholstered luxury of the back seat.

In this snug dining-room where chauffeur doubled as waiter, Jamshed lunched through his school days, safe from the vicissitudes of climate. The monsoon might drench the tiffin carriers to the bone and turn cold the boxes of 400 waiting schoolboys, but it could not touch Jamshed or his lunch. The tiffin carriers might arrive glistening and stinking of sweat in the hot season, with scorching hot tiffin boxes, hotter than they'd left the kitchens of Bombay, but Jamshed's lunch remained unaffected.

During the school years, my brother Percy spent many weekend afternoons at his friend's house. When he returned, Mother would commence the questioning: what did they eat? Was Jamshed's mother home? What did the two do all afternoon? Did they go out anywhere? And so on.

My brother did not confide in me very much in those days. Like all younger brothers, I was seen mainly as a nuisance. But my curiosity about Percy and Jamshed was satisfied by the interrogations. I knew that the afternoons were usually spent making model airplanes and listening to music. The airplanes were simple gliders in the early years; the music, mostly Mantovani and from Broadway shows. Later came more complex models with gasoline engines and remote control, and classical music from Bach to Poulenc.

The model airplanes were gifts from Jamshed's itinerant aunts and uncles, purchased during business trips to England or the U.S. Everyone except my brother and me seemed to have uncles and aunts smitten by wanderlust, and Jamshed's supply line from the western world guaranteed for him a steady diet of foreign clothes, shoes and records.

One Saturday, Percy reported during question period that Jamshed had just received the original soundtrack of *My Fair Lady.* This was sensational news. The LP was not available in Bombay, and a few privately imported or "smuggled" copies, brought in by people like Jamshed's relatives, were selling in the black market for 200 rupees. I had seen the records displayed side by side with foreign perfumes, chocolates and cheeses at the pavement stalls of "smugglers" along Flora Fountain.

After strenuous negotiations in which mother, Percy and I exhausted ourselves, he agreed to ask his friend if I could listen to the album. Arrangements were made. And next Saturday we set off for Jamshed's house. He welcomed me graciously, then put the record on the turntable.

The afternoon dragged by after the soundtrack finished. Bored, I watched them work on an airplane. The box said it was a Sopwith Camel. The name was familiar from the Biggles books Percy used to bring home. I picked up the lid and read dully that the aircraft had been designed by the British industrialist and aeronautical engineer, Thomas Octave Murdoch Sopwith, born 1888, and had been used during the First World War. Then followed a list of its parts.

Later, we had lunch, and talked. We talked of school, the school library, all the books that the library badly needed; and we talked of the *ghatis* who were flooding the school of late.

In the particular version of reality we inherited, *ghatis* were always flooding places, they never just went there. *Ghatis* were flooding the banks, desecrating the sanctity of institutions and taking up all the coveted jobs. *Ghatis* were even flooding the colleges and universities, a thing unheard of. Wherever you turned, the bloody *ghatis* were flooding the place.

With much shame I remember this word *ghati*. A suppurating sore of a word, oozing the stench of bigotry. It consigned a whole race to the mute roles of coolies and menials, forever unredeemable.

Once, as a child, I watched with detachment while a straining coolie loaded our family's baggage on his person during one of our rare vacations to Matheran. The big metal trunk he carried flat on his head, with the leather suitcase over it. The enormous hold-all he slung on his left arm, raised the arm to steady the load on his head and picked up the remaining suitcase with his right hand. This skeletal man then tottered off toward the train that would transport us to the little hill station. There, similar skeletal beings would be waiting with rickshaws. Automobiles were prohibited in Matheran, to preserve the pastoral purity of the place.

Many years later I found myself at the same hill station, a member of my college hikers' club, labouring up its slopes with a knapsack. Automobiles were still not permitted in Matheran, and every time a rickshaw sped by in a flurry of legs and wheels, we'd yell at the occupant: "Capitalist pig! Bastard! Stop riding on your brother's back!" The bewildered passenger would lean forward for a moment, not quite understanding, then fall back into the cushioned comfort of the rickshaw.

But this kind of smug socialism did not come till much later. First we had to reckon with school, school uniforms, brown paper covers for textbooks and exercise books, and the mad morning rush for the school bus. I remember how Percy used to rage and shout at the scrawny *ghaton* if the pathetic creature ever got in his way as she swept and mopped the floors. Mother would proudly observe, "He has a temper just like Grandpa's." She would also discreetly admonish Percy, since this was in the days when it was becoming quite difficult to find a new *ghaton*, especially if the first one quit due to abuse from the scion of the family and established her reasons for quitting amongst her colleagues. The good old days, when you could scream at a *ghaton* or even kick her and hurl her down the stairs and expect her to show up for work next morning, had definitely passed.

After high school, Percy and Jamshed went to different colleges. If they met at all, it would be at concerts of the Bombay Chamber Orchestra. With a group of college friends my brother organized a charitable agency that collected and distributed funds to destitute farmers in a small Maharashtian village. The idea was to get as many of these wretched souls as possible out of the clutches of the village moneylenders.

Jamshed showed a very superficial interest in what little he knew about Percy's activities. Each time they met, he would start with how he was trying his best to get out of the country. "Absolutely no future in this stupid place," he would say. "Bloody corruption everywhere. And you can't buy any of the things you want, don't even get to see a decent English movie. First chance I get, I'm going abroad. Preferably the U.S."

Jamshed did manage to leave. He came one day to say goodbye to Percy. But Percy was away working in his small village: the agency had taken on the task full time. Jamshed spoke to those of us who were home, and we all heartily agreed that he was doing the right thing. There just weren't any prospects in this country.

My parents announced that I, too, was trying to emigrate, but to Canada, not the U.S. "We will miss him if he gets to go," they told Jamshed, "but for the sake of his own future, he must. There is a lot of opportunity in Toronto. We've seen advertisements in newspapers from England, where Canadian Immigration is encouraging people to go to Canada. Of course they won't advertise in a country like India—who would want these bloody *ghatis* to come charging into their fine land?—but the office in New Delhi is holding interviews and selecting highly qualified applicants." According to my parents, I would have no difficulty being approved, what with my education, and my westernized background, and my fluency in the English language.

And they were right. A few months later, things were ready for my departure to Toronto.

But on my last night in Bombay, as I slept, a searing pain in my eyes woke me up. It was one o'clock. I bathed my eyes and tried to get back to sleep. Half-jokingly, I saw myself as someone out of a Greek tragedy, guilty of the sin of hubris for seeking emigration out of the land of my birth, and paying the price in burnt-out eyes: I Tiresias, blind and throbbing between two lives, the one in Bombay and the one to come in Toronto....

In the morning the doctor said it was conjunctivitis, nothing very serious. But I would need some drops every four hours and protective dark glasses till the infection was gone.

And so my last day in Bombay, the city of all my days till then, was spent in dark glasses. The last glimpse of my bed, my desk, my cricket bat, the chest of drawers I shared with Percy till he went away to the small village, came through dark glasses; the neighbourhood I grew up in, with the chemist's store ("Open 24 Hours"), the Irani restaurant, the sugarcane juice vendor, the fruit-and-vegetable stall, all of these I surveyed through dark glasses; the huddle of relatives at the airport, by the final barrier through which only ticket holders can pass, I waved to and saw one last time through dark glasses.

Tense with excitement, I walked across the tarmac. The slight chill I felt was due to the gusting night winds, I convinced myself. Then, eyes red with conjunctivitis, pocket bulging with the ridiculously large bottle of eye drops, and mind confused by a thousand half-formed thoughts and doubts, I boarded the aircraft.

After almost a year in Toronto I received a letter from Jamshed. From New York—a very neat missive, with an elegant little label showing his name and address. He wrote that he'd been to Bombay the previous month because in every single letter his mother had been pestering him to visit: "While there, I went to see your folks. Glad to hear you left India. But what about Percy? Can't understand what keeps him in that dismal place. He refuses to accept reality. All his efforts to help the farmers will be in vain. Nothing ever changes, just too much corruption. It's all part of the *ghati* mentality. I offered to help him immigrate if he ever changes his mind. I've got a lot of contacts now, in New York. But it's up to him to make up his mind," and on and on. Finally: "Bombay is horrible. Seems dirtier than ever, and the whole trip just made me sick. I had my fill of it in two weeks and was happy to leave." He ended with a cordial invitation to New York.

What I read was only the kind of stuff I would have expected in a letter from Jamshed. That was the way we all used to talk in Bombay. Still, it irritated me. It was puzzling that he could express so much disdain and discontentment even when he was no longer living under those conditions. Was it himself he was angry with, for not being able to come to terms with matters as Percy had? Was it because of the powerlessness that all of us experience who, mistaking weakness for strength, walk away from one thing or another?

I started a most punctilious reply to his letter. Very properly, I thanked him for visiting my parents and his concern for Percy. Equally properly, I reciprocated his invitation to New York with one to Toronto. Then, like a sly warlock adding an ingredient to his cauldron not called for in the recipe, I described the segment of Toronto's Gerrard Street known as Little India. I promised that when he visited, we would go to all the little restaurants there and gorge ourselves with *bhelpuri, panipuri, batata-wada, kulfi,* as authentic as any in Bombay; then we could browse through the shops selling imported spices and Hindi records, and maybe even see a Hindi movie at the Naaz Cinema. I often went to Little India, I wrote; he would be certain to have a great time.

The truth is, I have been there just once. And on that occasion I fled the place in a very short time, feeling extremely ill at ease and ashamed, wondering why all this did not make me feel homesick or at least a little nostalgic. But Jamshed did not have to know any of it. My letter must have told him that whatever he suffered from, I did not share it. For a long time afterwards I did not hear from him.

My days were always full. I attended evening classes at the University of Toronto, desultorily gathering philosophy credits, and worked during the day. I became a member of the Zoroastrian Society of Ontario. Hoping to meet people from Bombay, I also went to the Parsee New Year celebrations and dinner.

The event was held at a community centre rented for the occasion. As the evening progressed it took on, at an alarming rate, the semblance of a wedding party at Bombay's Cama Baag, as we Parsees talked at the top of our voices, embraced heartily, drank heartily and ate heartily. It was Cama Baag refurbished and modernized, Cama Baag without the cluster of beggars by the entrance gate, waiting for the feast to end so they could come in and claim the dustbins.

My membership in the Society led to dinner invitations at Parsee homes. The guests at these gatherings were not the type who would be regulars at Little India, but who might go there with the air of tourists, equipped with a supply of ohs and aahs for ejaculation at suitable moments, pretending to discover what they had always lived with.

These were people who knew all about the different airlines that flew to Bombay. These were the virtuosi of transatlantic travel. If someone inquired of the most recent traveller, "How was your trip to India?" another would be ready with "What airline?" The evening would then become a convention of travel agents expounding the salient features of their preferred carriers.

After a few such copiously educational evenings, I knew what the odds were of my luggage getting lost if I travelled airline A. The best food was served on airline B. Departures were always delayed with airline C (the company had a *ghati* sense of time and punctuality, they said). The washrooms were filthy and blocked up on airline D (no fault of airline D, they explained, it was the low class of public that travelled on it).

Of Bombay itself the conversation was restricted to the shopping they'd done. They brought back tales of villainous shopkeepers who tried to cheat them because they sensed that here was the affluence of foreign exchange: "Very cunning, they all are. God knows how, but they are able to smell your dollars before you even open your wallet. Then they try to fool you in the way they fool all the other tourists. I used to tell them"—this, in broken Hindi—"'go, go, what you thinking, I someone new in Mumbai? I living here 30 years, yes 30, before going foreign.' Then they would bargain sensibly."

Others told of the way they had made a shrewd deal with shopkeepers who did not know the true value of brass and copper artifacts and knickknacks. These collector of bric-a-brac, self-appointed connoisseurs of art and antiques, must have acquired their fancies along with their immigration visas. But their number was small. They never quite succeeded in holding the gathering transfixed the way the airline clique managed to. Art was not as popular as airlines were at these evenings.

Six months after Jamshed's trip to Bombay, I received a letter from my brother Percy. Among other things, he wrote about his commitment in the small village:

Our work with the farmers started successfully. They got interest-free loans in the form of seed and fertilizer, which we purchased wholesale, and for the first time in years they did not have to borrow from those bloodthirsty moneylenders.

Ever since we got there the moneylenders hated us. They tried to persuade us to leave, saying that what we were doing was wrong because it was upsetting the delicate balance of village life and destroying tradition. We in turn pointed out things like exploitation, usury, inhumanity and other abominations whose time was now up. We may have sounded like bold knights-errant, but they turned to threats and said it would soon become so unhealthy for us that we would leave quickly enough.

One day when we were out visiting a loan applicant, a farmer who lived close to us brought news that a gang of thugs wielding sticks and cudgels was waiting at the hut —our office and residence. So we stayed the night with the loan applicant and, in the morning, escorted by a band of villagers who insisted on coming along, started for our hut. But all we found were smouldering embers. It had been razed to the ground during the night, and no-one had dared interfere.

Now we're back in Bombay, working on a plan for our return. We've spoken to several reporters, and the work is getting much publicity. We're also collecting fresh donations, so that when we go back we won't fail for lack of funds.

Having read this far, I put down the letter for a moment. There you were, my brother, waging battle against corruption and evil, while I was watching sitcoms on my rented Granada TV and attending dinner parties at Parsee homes to listen to chitchat about airlines and trinkets.

The rest of the letter concerned Jamshed's visit to Bombay six months ago:

> I wish he'd stayed away, if not from Bombay then at least from me. At best, the time I spent with him was a waste. I expected that we would look at things differently, but was not prepared for the crassly materialistic boor that he's turned into. To think he was my "best friend" in school.
>
> No doubt he believes the highlight of his visit came when he took some of us to dinner at the Rendezvous—nothing but the most expensive, of course. It was a spectacle to surpass anything he'd done so far. He reminded us to eat and drink as much as we wanted without minding the prices, to enjoy ourselves as much as we could, because we wouldn't get such a chance again, at least, not until his next visit.
>
> When the soup came he scolded the waiter that it was cold and sent it back. The rest of us sat silent and embarrassed. He looked at us nonchalantly, explaining that this was the only way to handle incompetence; Indians were too meek and docile, and should learn to stand up for their rights the way people do in the States.
>
> We were supposed to be impressed by his performance, for we were in an expensive restaurant where only foreign tourists eat on the strength of their U.S. dollars. And here was one of our own, not intimidated within the walls of the five-star Taj Mahal Hotel. In our school days we could only stand outside and watch the foreigners come and go, wondering what opulent secrets lay inside, what comforts these fair-skinned superior beings enjoyed. Here was one of our own showing us how to handle it all without feeling a trace of inferiority.
>
> We spent the evening watching Jamshed in disbelief, in silence, which he probably thought was due to the awesome splendour of our surroundings.

I was determined not to see him again, not even when he came to say goodbye on the day of his departure, and I don't intend to meet him when he visits Bombay the next time....

As I finished reading, I felt that my brother had been as irritated by Jamshed's presence as I had been by Jamshed's letter six months ago. But I did not write this to Percy. After all, I was planning to be in Bombay in four or five months. We could talk then. In just four more months I would complete two years in Canada—long enough a separation, I supposed with a naïve pomposity, to develop a lucidity of thought that I would carry back with me and bring to bear on all of India's problems.

Soon it was time to go shopping for gifts. I packed my suitcases with chocolates, cheeses, jams, jellies, puddings, cake mixes, panty hose, stainless steel razor blades—all the items I used to see displayed in the stalls of the "smugglers" along Flora Fountain, always priced out of reach. I felt like one of those soldiers who, in wartime, accumulates strange things to use as currency for barter.

Then, arms still sore from the typhoid and cholera inoculations, luggage bursting at the seams with a portable grocery store and mind suffused with groundless optimism, I boarded the plane.

The aircraft was losing height in preparation for landing. The hard afternoon sun revealed the city I was coming back to after two years. When the plane had taken off two years ago, it had been in the dark of night, and all I saw from the sky through shaded and infected eyes were the airport lights of Santa Cruz. But now it was daylight, and I was not wearing dark glasses. I could see the parched land: brown, weary and unhappy.

A few hours earlier the aircraft had made its scheduled

landing in London, and the view from the air had been lush, everywhere green and hopeful. It enraged me as I contrasted it with what I was now seeing. Gone was the clearness with which I'd promised myself I would look at things. All that was left was a childish and helpless reaction. "It's not fair!" I wanted to stamp my foot and shout. "It's just not fair!"

Bombay seemed dirtier than ever. I remembered what Jamshed had written in his letter, and how it had annoyed me. Hostility and tension seemed to be perpetually present in buses, shops, trains, all teeming with people. It was disconcerting to discover I'd become unused to it. Now I knew what soldiers must experience in the trenches after a respite far behind the lines.

As if enacting a scene for my benefit, a crowd clawed its way into a local train. Someone dropped a plastic lunch bag amidst the stampede. When the train departed, the owner matter-of-factly picked up the mangled lunch, dusted off a chapati that had slipped out of the trampled bag, and waited for the next train. It was as if, in the man's resignation, there was a lesson for me: to trim my expectations and reactions to things, trim them down to the proper proportions, make them suit this reality.

After this, I felt I could fit right in. The first flush of confidence appeared when I missed my bus. The old instinctive impulse returned, to dash after it, to leap and join the crowd already hanging from the door rail. In the old days I would have been off and running. I used to take pride in my agility at this manoeuvre. After all, during rush hour it was the only way to catch a bus, or you'd be left at the bus stop with the old and the feeble. It was just one more trick acquired to keep ahead in the daily struggle for survival.

But the bus had moved well into the flow of traffic. My momentary hesitation gave the game away. With the old and feeble was my place, as long as I was a tourist here, and not committed to life in the combat zone.

My brother Percy wrote from the small village that he wanted to meet me, but: "I cannot come to Bombay right now because I've received a letter from Jamshed. He's flying in from New York, and has written about reunions and great times for all the old crowd. That's out of the question as far as I'm concerned. I'm not going to see him again."

I wrote back saying I understood.

Our parents were disappointed. They had been so happy that the whole family would be together again for a while. And now this. They could not understand why Percy did not like Jamshed any more, and I'm sure at the back of their minds they thought their son was envious of his friend because of the fine success he'd made of himself in America. If only they knew the truth. But who was I to explain things, and would they understand even if I tried? They truly believed that Jamshed was the smart young fellow, and Percy the idealist who forgot that charity begins at home.

This trip was not turning out to be anything I'd hoped it would. Jamshed was coming and Percy wasn't, our parents were disappointed with Percy, I was disappointed with them, and in a week I would be flying out of Bombay, confused and miserable. I could feel it already.

Without any destination in mind I left the house and took the first empty bus to come along. It went to Flora Fountain. The offices were now closing for the day. The dirty, yellow-grey buildings would soon spill out typists and clerks and peons into a swelling stream surging toward bus stops and train stations.

Roadside stalls were open for business. This would be their busy hour. They were lined up along the edge of the pavement, displaying their merchandise. Here a profusion of towels and napkins from shocking pink to peacock green; there, the clatter and gleam of pots and pans; further down, a refreshment stall selling sizzling *samosas* and ice-cold sherbet.

The pavement across the road was the domain of the "smugglers" with their stalls of foreign goods. But they did not interest me, I stayed where I was. One man was peddling an assortment of toys. He demonstrated them all in turn, calling out, "Baba play and baby play! Daddy play and Mummy play!" Another, with fiendish vigour, was throwing glass bowls to the ground, yelling: "Un-ber-rakable! Un-ber-rakable!"

Sunlight began to fade as I listened to the hawkers singing their tunes. Kerosene lamps were lit in some of the stalls, punctuating at random the rows on both sides of the street.

Serenely I stood and watched. The disappointment that had overcome me earlier began to ebb. All was fine and warm within this moment after sunset, when the lanterns were lit. I began to feel a part of the crowds that were now flowing down Flora Fountain. I walked with them.

Suddenly, a hand on my shoulder made me turn around. It was Jamshed. "Bet you weren't expecting to see me in Bombay."

"Actually, I was. Percy wrote you were coming." Then I wished I hadn't volunteered this bit of information.

But there was no need to worry about awkward questions regarding Percy. For Jamshed, in fine fettle, had other thoughts he was anxious to share.

"So what are you doing here? Come shopping?" he jokingly asked, indicating the little stalls with a disdainful sweep of his hand. "Terrible, isn't it, the way the buggers think they own the streets—don't even leave you enough room to walk. The police should drive them off, break up their bloody stalls, really."

He paused. I wondered if I should say something. Something that Percy would love to hear me say. Like: these people were only trying to earn a meagre living, exercising, amidst a paucity of options, this one; at least they were not begging or stealing.

But I didn't have a chance. "God, what a racket! Impossible to take even a quiet little walk in this place. I tell you, I'll be happy when it's time to catch my plane back to New York."

It was hopeless. It was his letter all over again, the one he'd written the year before from New York. He had then temporarily disturbed the order I was trying to bring into my new life in Toronto, and I'd struck back with a letter of my own. But this time I just wanted to get away from him as quickly as possible. Before he made the peace of mind I was reaching out for dissipate, become forever unattainable.

Suddenly, I understood why Percy did not want to meet him again—he, too, sensed and feared Jamshed's soul-sapping presence.

Around us, all the pavement stalls were immersed in a rich dusk. Each one was now lit by a flickering kerosene lantern. What could I say to Jamshed? What would it take, I wondered, to light the lantern in his soul?

He was waiting for me to speak. I asked, perfunctorily, how much longer he would be in Bombay.

"Another week. Seven whole days, and they'll go so slowly. But I'll be dropping in at your place in a couple of days, tell Percy." We walked to my bus stop and said goodnight.

On the bus I thought about what to say if he asked me, two days later, why I hadn't mentioned that Percy was not coming.

As it turned out, I did not have to say anything.

Late next evening, Percy came home unexpectedly. I rushed to greet him, but his face revealed that he was not returning in this manner as part of a pleasantly planned surprise. Something was dreadfully wrong. His colour was ashen. He was frightened and shaken, and struggled to retain his composure. He tried to smile as he shook my hand limply, but could not muster the effort to return my hug.

"What's the matter?" said Mother. "You don't look well."

Silently, Percy sat down and began to remove his shoes and socks. After a while he looked up and said, "They killed Navjeet."

No-one spoke for the next few minutes. Percy sat with his socks dangling from his hands, looking sad, tired, defeated.

Then Mother rose and said she would make tea. Over tea, he told us what had happened. Slowly, reluctantly at first, then faster, in a rush, to get the remembering and telling over with as fast as possible. "When we returned to the village the moneylenders were there to make trouble for us. We didn't think they'd do anything as serious as the last time. The press was following our progress and had reported the arson in many newspapers. Yesterday we were out at the wholesaler's. Ordering seed for next year. But Navjeet had stayed behind. He was working on the accounts. When we returned he was lying unconscious. On the floor. His face and head were bleeding badly. We carried him to the makeshift clinic in the village—there is no hospital. The doctor said there was severe internal damage—massive head injuries—a few hours later he was dead."

There was silence again. Perhaps when we were together sharing our old room, Percy would talk to me. But in the darkness he lay wide awake, staring silently at the ceiling, tracing its old familiar cracks, as I was, by the hints of streetlights straying through the curtained window. Was there nothing to say? There must be something I could do to help.

Strangely enough, it was Jamshed who provided this something. Quite unwittingly, of course.

When he arrived in the evening, Mother asked him how he'd been enjoying his trip so far. He replied, true to form, "Oh Auntie, I'm tired of this place, really. The dust and heat and crowds—I've had enough of it." And Mother nodded sympathetically.

Soon, the moment Percy had been dreading was at hand. Mother asked him to narrate, for Jamshed's benefit, the events that had brought him home so suddenly. But Percy just shook his head, so she told the story herself.

When she finished, Jamshed could not contain himself. He heaved the sigh of the worldly-wise: "I told you from the beginning, all this was a waste of time and nothing would come of it, remember? I still think the best thing for you is to come to the States. There is so much you could achieve there. There, if you are good at something, you are appreciated, and you get ahead. Not like here, where everything is controlled by Uncle-Auntie, and...."

I watched my brother, certain that he would finally allow his exasperation with Jamshed to spill, and say all the things that were choking him.

But when Jamshed concluded his harangue, Percy calmly turned to Mother and said in his quiet voice, "Could we have dinner right away? I have to meet my friends at eight o'clock. To decide our next move in the village."

Five days later I was back in Toronto. Gradually, I discovered I'd brought back with me my entire burden of riddles and puzzles, unsolved. The whole sorry package was there, not lightened at all. The epiphany would have to wait for another time, another trip.

I mused, I gave way to whimsy: I Tiresias, throbbing between two lives, humbled by the ambiguities and dichotomies confronting me....

I thought of Jamshed and his adamant refusal to enjoy his trips to India, his way of seeing the worst in everything. Was he, too, waiting for some epiphany and growing impatient because, without it, life in America was bewildering? Perhaps the contempt and disdain that he shed was only his way of lightening his own load.

That Christmas, I received a card from Jamshed. The Christmas seal, postage stamp, address label were all neatly and correctly in place upon the envelope, like everything else about his surface existence. I put it down without opening it, wondering if this innocuous outer shell concealed more of his confusion, disdain, arrogance.

Later, I walked out of the apartment and down the hallway, and dropped the envelope down the chute of the garbage incinerator.

The Collectors

I

When Dr. Burjor Mody was transferred from Mysore to assume the principalship of the Bombay Veterinary College, he moved into Pherozeshah Baag with his wife and son Pesi. They occupied the vacant flat on the third floor of C Block, next to the Bulsara family.

Dr. Mody did not know it then, but he would be seeing a lot of Jehangir, the Bulsara boy. The boy who sat silent and brooding, every evening, watching the others at play, and called *chaarikhao* by them—quite unfairly, since he never tattled or told tales (Dr. Mody would call him, affectionately, the observer of C Block). And Dr. Mody did not know this, either, at the time of moving, that Jehangir Bulsara's visits at ten o'clock every Sunday morning would become a source of profound joy for himself. Or that just when he would think he had found someone to share his hobby with, someone to mitigate the perpetual disappointment about his son Pesi, he would lose his precious Spanish dancing-lady stamp and renounce Jehangir's friendship, both in quick succession. And then two years later, he himself would—but *that* is never knowable.

Soon after moving in, Dr. Burjor Mody became the pride of the Parsees in C Block. C Block, like the rest of Pherozeshah Baag, had a surfeit of low-paid bank clerks and bookkeepers, and the arrival of Dr. Mody permitted them to feel a little better about themselves. More important, in A Block lived a prominent priest, and B Block boasted a chartered accountant. Now C Block had a voice in Baag matters as important as the others did.

While C Block went about its routine business, confirming and authenticating the sturdiness of the object of their pride, the doctor's big-boned son Pesi established himself as leader of the rowdier elements among the Baag's ten-to-sixteen population. For Pesi, too, it was routine business; he was following a course he had mapped out for himself ever since the family began moving from city to city on the whims and megrims of his father's employer, the government.

To account for Pesi's success was the fact of his brutish strength. But he was also the practitioner of a number of minor talents that appealed to the crowd where he would be leader. The one no doubt complemented the other, the talents serving to dissemble the brutish qualifier of strength, and the brutish strength encouraging the crowd to perceive the appeal of his talents.

Hawking, for instance, was one of them. Pesi could summon up prodigious quantities of phlegm whenever he wanted to, accompanied by sounds such as the boys had seldom heard except in accomplished adults: deep, throaty, rasping, resonating rolls that culminated in a pthoo, with the impressive trophy landing in the dust at their feet, its size leaving them all slightly envious. Pesi could also break wind that sounded like questions, exclamations, fragments of the chromatic scale and clarion calls, while the others sniffed and discussed the merits of pungency versus tonality. This ability had earned him the appellation of Pesi *paad-maroo,* and he wore the sobriquet with pride.

Perhaps Pesi's single most important talent was his ability to improvise. The peculiarities of a locale were the raw material for his inventions. In Pherozeshah Baag, behind the buildings, were spacious yards shared by all three blocks. Till the arrival of the Mody family, these yards were home for stray and happy cats, well fed on scraps and leftovers disgorged regularly as clockwork, after mealtimes, by the three blocks of Pherozeshah Baag. The ground floors were the only ones who refrained. They voiced their protests in a periodic cycle of reasoning, pleading and screaming of obscenities, because the garbage collected outside their windows. If the cascade of food was more than the cats would devour, the remainder fell to the fortune of the rats. Finally, flies and insects buzzed and hovered over the dregs, little pools of pulses and curries fermenting and frothing, till the *kuchrawalli* came next morning and swept it all away.

The backyards of Pherozeshah Baag gave Pesi the idea for a new game: stoning-the-cats. The boys gathered at the rear windows of their homes, preferably at a time of day when the adults were scarce, with the fathers away at work and the mothers not yet finished with their afternoon naps. Each boy brought a pile of small stones and took turns, chucking three stones each. The game could just as easily have been stoning-the-rats; but stoned rats quietly walked away to safety, whereas the yowls of cats provided primal satisfaction and verified direct hits—no yowl, no point. The game was a success, and added to Pesi's popularity. But the parents (except the ground floor) complained to Dr. Mody about his son instigating their children to torment poor dumb and helpless creatures. For a veterinarian's son to harass animals was shameful, they said.

As might be supposed, Pesi was the despair of his parents. Over the years Dr. Mody had become inured to the initial embarrassment in each new place they moved to. The routine was familiar: first, a spate of complaints from indignant parents claiming their sons *bugree ney dhoor thai gaya*—were corrupted to become useless as dust; next, the protestations giving way to sympathy when the neighbours saw that Pesi was the worm in the Modys' mango.

And so it was in Pherozeshah Baag. After the furor about stoning-the-cats had died down, the people of the Baag liked Dr. Mody more than ever. He earned their respect for the initiative he took in Baag matters, dealing with the management for things like broken lifts, leaking water tanks, crumbling plaster and faulty wiring. It was at his urging that the massive iron gate was repaired and a watchman installed to stop beggars and riffraff. (And although Dr. Mody would be dead by the time of the *Shiv Sena* riots, the tenants would remember him for the gate that would keep out the rampaging mobs.) When the Bombay Municipality tried to appropriate a section of Baag property for its road-widening scheme, Dr. Mody was in the forefront of the battle, winning a compromise whereby the Baag lost only half the proposed area. But the Baag's esteem did nothing to lighten the despair for Pesi that hung around the doctor.

At the birth of his son, Dr. Mody had deliberated long and hard about the naming. Peshotan, in the Persian epic, *Shah-Nameh,* was the brother of the great Asfandyar, and a noble general, lover of art and learning, and man of wise counsel. Dr. Mody had decided his son would play the violin, acquire the best from the cultures of East and West, thrill to the words of Tagore and Shakespeare, appreciate Mozart and Indian ragas; and one day, at the proper moment, he would introduce him to his dearest activity, stamp-collecting.

But the years passed in their own way. Fate denied fruition to all of Dr. Mody's plans, and when he talked about stamps Pesi laughed and mocked his beloved hobby. This was the point at which, hurt and confused, he surrendered his son to whatever destiny was in store. A perpetual grief entered to occupy the void left behind after the aspirations for his son were evicted.

The weight of grief was heaviest around Dr. Mody when he returned from work in the evenings. As his car turned into the compound, he usually saw Pesi before Pesi saw him, in scenes that made him despair, scenes in which his son was abusing someone, fighting or making lewd gestures. But Dr. Mody was careful not to make a public spectacle of his despair. While the car made its way sluggishly over the uneven flagstones of the compound, the boys would stand back and wave him through. With his droll comments and jovial countenance he was welcome to disrupt their play, unlike the other two car-owners of Pherozeshah Baag: the priest in A Block and the chartered accountant in B who habitually berated, from inside their vehicles, the sons of bank clerks and bookkeepers for blocking the driveway with their games. Their well-worn cries and curses had become so predictable and ineffective that sometimes the boys chanted gleefully, in unison, with their nemeses: "Worse than *saala* animals!" or "*Junglee* dogs-cats have more sense!" or "You *saetaans* ever have any lesson-*paani* to do or not!"

There was one boy who always stayed apart from his peers—the Bulsara boy, from the family next door to the Modys. Jehangir sat on the stone steps every evening while the gentle land breezes, drying and cooling the sweaty skins of the boys at play, blew out to sea. He sat alone through the long dusk, a source of discomfiture to the others. They resented his melancholy, watching presence.

Dr. Mody noticed Jehangir, too, on the stone steps of C Block, the delicate boy with the build much too slight for his age. Next to a hulk like Pesi he was diminutive, but things other than size underlined his frail looks. He had slender hands, and forearms with fine downy hair. While facial fuzz was incipient in most boys of his age, and Pesi was positively hirsute, Jehangir's chin and upper lip were smooth as a young woman's. But it pleased Dr. Mody to see him evening after evening. The quiet contemplation of the boy on the steps and the noise and activity of the others at play came together in the kind of balance that Dr. Mody was always looking for and was quick to appreciate.

Jehangir, in his turn, observed the burly Dr. Mody closely as he walked past him each evening. When he approached the steps after parking his car, Jehangir would say "*Sahibji*" in greeting, and smile wanly. He saw that despite Dr. Mody's constant jocularity there was something painfully empty about his eyes. He noticed the peculiar way he scratched the greyish-red patches of psoriasis on his elbows, both elbows simultaneously, by folding his arms across his chest. Sometimes Jehangir would arise from the stone steps and the two would go up together to the third floor. Dr. Mody asked him once, "You don't like playing with the other boys? You just sit and watch them?" The boy shook his head and blushed, and he did not bring up the matter after that.

Gradually, a friendship of sorts grew between the two. Jehangir touched a chord inside the doctor that had lain silent for much too long. Now affection for the boy developed and started to linger around the region hitherto occupied by grief bearing Pesi's name.

2

One evening, while Jehangir sat on the stone steps waiting for Dr. Mody's car to arrive, Pesi was organizing a game of *naargolio.* He divided the boys into two teams, then discovered he was one short. He beckoned to the epicene Jehangir, who said he did not want to play. Scowling, Pesi handed the ball to one of the others and walked over to him. He grabbed his collar with both hands, jerking him to his feet. "*Arré chussiya!* Want a pasting?" he yelled, and began dragging him by the collar to where the boys had piled up the seven flat stones for *naargolio.*

At that instant, Dr. Mody's car turned into the compound, and he spied his son in one of those scenes that made him despair. But today the despair was swept aside by rage when he saw that Pesi's victim was Jehangir Bulsara. He left the car in the middle of the compound with the motor running. Anger glinted in his eyes. He kicked over the pile of seven flat stones as he walked blindly toward Pesi who, having seen his father, had released Jehangir. He had been caught by his father often enough to know that it was best to stand and wait. Jehangir, meanwhile, tried to keep back the tears.

Dr. Mody stopped before his son and slapped him hard, once on each cheek, with the front and back of his right hand. He waited, as if debating whether that was enough, then put his arm around Jehangir and led him to the car.

He drove to his parking spot. By now, Jehangir had control of his tears, and they walked to the steps of C Block. The lift was out of order. They climbed the stairs to the third floor and knocked. He waited with Jehangir.

Jehangir's mother came to the door. "*Sahibji,* Dr. Mody," she said, a short, middle-aged woman, very prim, whose hair was always in a bun. Never without a *maathabana,* she could do wonderful things with that square of fine white cloth that was tied and knotted to sit like a cap on her head, snugly packeting the bun. In the evenings, after the household chores were done, she removed the *maathabana* and wore it in a more conventional manner, like a scarf. "*Sahibji,*" she said, then noticed her son's tear-stained face. "*Arré,* Jehangoo, what happened, who made you cry?" Her hand flew automatically to the *maathabana,* tugging and adjusting it as she did whenever she was concerned or agitated.

To save the boy embarrassment Dr. Mody intervened: "Go, wash your face while I talk to your mother." Jehangir went inside, and Dr. Mody told her briefly about what had happened. "Why does he not play with the other boys?" he asked finally.

"Dr. Mody, what to say. The boy never wants even to go out. *Khoedai salaamat raakhé,* wants to sit at home all the time and read storybooks. Even this little time in the evening he goes because I force him and tell him he will not grow tall without fresh air. Every week he brings new-new storybooks from school. First, school library would allow only one book per week. But he went to Father Gonzalves who is in charge of library and got special permission for two books. God knows why he gave it."

"But reading is good, Mrs. Bulsara."

"I know, I know, but a mania like this, all the time?"

"Some boys are the outdoor type, some are indoor type. You shouldn't worry about Jehangir, he is a very good boy. Look at my Pesi, now there is a case for worry," he said, meaning to reassure her.

"No, no. You mustn't say that. Be patient, *Khoedai* is great," said Mrs. Bulsara, consoling him instead. Jehangir returned, his eyes slightly red but dry. While washing his face he had wet a lock of his hair that hung down over his forehead.

"Ah, here comes my indoor champion," smiled Dr. Mody, and patted Jehangir's shoulder, brushing back the lock of hair. Jehangir did not understand, but grinned anyway; the doctor's joviality was infectious. Dr. Mody turned again to the mother. "Send him to my house on Sunday at ten o'clock. We will have a little talk."

After Dr. Mody left, Jehangir's mother told him how lucky he was that someone as important and learned as Burjor Uncle was taking an interest in him. Privately she hoped he would encourage the boy toward a more all-rounded approach to life and do the things other boys did. And when Sunday came she sent Jehangir off to Dr. Mody's promptly at ten.

Dr. Mody was taking his bath, and Mrs. Mody opened the door. She was a dour-faced woman, spare and lean—the opposite of her husband in appearance and disposition, yet retaining some quality from long ago that suggested that it had not always been so. Jehangir had never crossed her path save when she was exchanging civilities with his mother while making purchases, out by the stairs, from the vegetablewalla or fruitwalla.

Not expecting Jehangir's visit, Mrs. Mody stood blocking the doorway and said "Yes?" meaning, what nuisance now?

"Burjor Uncle asked me to come at ten o'clock."

"Asked you to come at ten o'clock? What for?"

"He just said to come at ten o'clock."

Grudgingly, Mrs. Mody stepped aside. "Come in then. Sit down there." And she indicated the specific chair she wanted him to occupy, muttering something about a *baap* who had time for strangers' children but not for his own son.

Jehangir sat in what must have been the most uncomfortable chair in the room. This was his first time inside the Modys' flat, and he looked around with curiosity. But his gaze was quickly restricted to the area of the floor directly in front of him when he realized that he was the object of Mrs. Mody's watchfulness.

Minutes ticked by under the vigilant eye of Mrs. Mody. Jehangir was grateful when Dr. Mody emerged from the bedroom. Being Sunday, he had eschewed his usual khaki half-pants for loose and comfortable white pyjamas. His *sudra* hung out over it, and he strode vigorously, feet encased in a huge pair of *sapaat.* He smiled broadly, and Jehangir happily noted the crow's-feet appearing at the corners of his eyes. He was ushered into Dr. Mody's room, and man and boy both seemed glad to escape the surveillance of the woman.

The chairs were more comfortable in Dr. Mody's room. They sat at his desk and Dr. Mody opened a drawer to take out a large book.

"This was the first stamp album I ever had," said Dr. Mody. "It was given to me by my Nusserwanji Uncle when I was your age. All the pages were empty." He began turning them. Every page was covered with stamps, each a feast of colour and design. He talked as he turned the pages, and

Jehangir watched and listened, glancing at the stamps flying past, at Dr. Mody's face, then at the stamps again. Dr. Mody spoke, not in his usual booming, jovial tones but softly, in a low voice charged with inspiration. The stamps whizzed by, and his speech was underlined gently by the rustle of the heavily laden pages that seemed to turn of their own volition in the quiet room. (Jehangir would remember this peculiar rustle when one day, older, he'd stand alone in this very room, silenced now forever, and turn the pages of Nusserwanji Uncle's album.) Jehangir watched and listened. It was as if a mask had descended over Dr. Mody, a faraway look upon his face and a shining in the eyes that heretofore Jehangir had only seen sad with despair or glinting with anger or just plain and empty, and belying his constant drollery. Jehangir watched, and listened to the euphonious voice hinting at wondrous things and promises and dreams.

The album on the desk, able to produce such changes in Dr. Mody, now worked its magic upon the boy. Jehangir, watching and listening, fascinated, tried to read the names of the countries at the top of the pages as they sped by: Antigua...Australia...Belgium...Bhutan...Bulgaria...and on through to Malta and Mauritius...Romania and Russia ...Togo and Tonga, and a final blur through which he caught Yugoslavia and Zanzibar.

"Can I see it again?" he asked, and Dr. Mody handed the album to him.

"So what do you think? Do you want to be a collector?"

Jehangir nodded eagerly and Dr. Mody laughed. "When Nusserwanji Uncle showed me his collection I felt just like that. I'll tell your mother what to buy for you to get you started. Bring it here next Sunday."

And next Sunday Jehangir was ready by nine. He waited by the door with a Stamp Album for Beginners and a packet of 100 Assorted Stamps—All Countries. Going too early would mean sitting under the baleful eyes of Mrs. Mody.

Ten o'clock struck and the clock's tenth bong was echoed by the Modys' doorchimes. Mrs. Mody was expecting him this time and did not block the doorway. Wordlessly, she beckoned him in. Burjor Uncle was ready, too, and came out almost immediately to rescue him from her arena.

"Let's see what you've got there," he said when they were in his room. They removed the cellophane wrapper, and while they worked Dr. Mody enjoyed himself as much as the boy. His deepest wish appeared to be coming true—he had at last found someone to share his hobby with; he could not have hoped for a finer young recruit than Jehangir.

When it was almost time to leave, Jehangir asked if he could examine again Nusserwanji Uncle's album, the one he had seen last Sunday. But Burjor Uncle led him instead to a cupboard in the corner of the room. "Since you enjoy looking at my stamps, let me show you what I have here." He unlocked its doors.

Each of the cupboard's four shelves were piled with biscuit-tins and sweet-tins—round, oval, rectangular, square. They bore the unmistakable stamp of the worthless hoardings of senility, and it puzzled Jehangir. But Burjor Uncle reached out for one and showed him inside. It was chock-full of stamps! Jehangir's mouth fell open. He gaped at the shelves and Burjor Uncle laughed. "All these tins are full of stamps. And that big cardboard box at the bottom contains six new albums, all empty."

Jehangir tried to assign a number to the stamps in the containers of Maghanlal Biscuitwalla and N. Lokmanji Mithaiwalla, to all of the stamps in the round tins and the oval tins, the square ones and the oblong ones. He failed.

Once again Dr. Mody laughed at the boy's wonderment. "A lot of stamps. And they took me a lot of years to collect. Of course, I am lucky I have many contacts in foreign countries. Because of my job, I meet the experts from abroad who are invited by the Indian Government. When I tell them about my hobby, they send me stamps from their countries. But I have no time to sort them so I pack them into boxes. One day, after I retire, I will spend all my time with my stamps." He paused, and shut the cupboard doors. "So what you have to do now is start making lots of friends, tell them about your hobby. If they also collect, you can exchange duplicates with them. If they don't, you can still ask them for stamps. You do something for them, they will do something for you. Your collection will grow depending on how smart you are."

He hesitated, opened the cupboard again. Then he changed his mind and shut it—it wasn't yet time for the Spanish dancing-lady stamp.

3

On the pavement outside St. Xavier's Boys School stood two variety stalls. They were the stalls of *Patla Babu* and *Jhaaria Babu.* Their real names were never known. Nor was known the source of the inspiration that named them thus, after their respective thinness and fatness.

Before the schoolboys arrived in the morning, the two would unpack their cases and set up the displays, beating the beggars to the choice positions. There were occasional disputes if someone's space was violated. The beggars did not harbour great hopes for alms from schoolboys but they stood there, nonetheless, mute lessons in realism and the harshness of life. Their patience was rewarded when they raided the dustbins after breaks and lunches.

At the end of the school day the pavement community packed up. The beggars shuffled off into the approaching dark, *Patla Babu* went home with his cases, and *Jhaaria Babu* slept near the school gate under a large tree to whose trunk he chained his boxes during the night.

The two sold a variety of nondescript objects and comestibles, uninteresting to any save the eyes and stomachs of schoolboys: *supari,* A-1 chewing gum (which, in a most ungumlike manner, would, after a while, dissolve in one's mouth), *jeeragoli,* marbles, tops, *aampapad* during the mango season, pens, Camel Ink, pencils, rulers and stamps in little cellophane packets.

Patla Babu and *Jhaaria Babu* lost some of their goods regularly due to theft. This was inevitable when doing business outside a large school like St. Xavier's, with a population as varied as its was. The loss was an operating expense stoically accepted, like the success or failure of the monsoons, and they never complained to the school authorities or held it against the boys. Besides, business was good despite the losses: insignificant items like a packet of *jeeragoli* worth ten paise, or a marble of the kind that sold three for five paise. More often than not, the stealing went on for the excitement of it, out of bravado or on a dare. It was called "flicking" and was done without any malice toward *Patla* and *Jhaaria.*

Foremost among the flickers was a boy in Jehangir's class called Eric D'Souza. He was a tall, lanky fellow who had failed a couple of times, had had to repeat the year on two occasions and held out the promise of more repetitions. Eric also had the reputation of doing things inside his half-pants under cover of his desk. In a class of fifty boys it was easy to go unobserved by the teacher, and only his immediate neighbours could see the ecstasy on his face and the vigorous back and forth movement of his hand. When he grinned at them they looked away, pretending not to have noticed anything.

Jehangir sat far from Eric and knew of his habits only by hearsay. He was oblivious to Eric's eye, which had been on him for quite a while. In fact, Eric found his delicate hands and fingers, his smooth legs and thighs very desirable. In class he gazed for hours, longingly, at the girlish face, curly hair, long eyelashes.

Jehangir finally made his acquaintance one day when the class filed out for games period. Eric had been made to kneel down by the door for coming late and disturbing the class, and Jehangir found himself next to him as he stood in line. Eric looked up from his kneeling position at the smooth thighs emerging from the half-pants (half-pants was the school uniform requirement), winked at him and, unhindered by underwear, inserted a pencil up the pant leg. He tickled Jehangir's genitals seductively with the eraser end, expertly, then withdrew it. Jehangir feigned a giggle, too shocked to say anything. The line started to move for the playground.

Shortly after this incident, Eric approached Jehangir during breaktime. He had heard that Jehangir was desperate to acquire stamps.

"*Arré* man, I can get you stamps, whatever kind you want," he said.

Jehangir stopped. He had been slightly confused ever since that pass with the pencil; Eric frightened him a little with his curious habits and forbidden knowledge. But it had not been easy to accumulate stamps. Sundays with Burjor Uncle continued to be as fascinating as the first. He wished he had new stamps to show—the stasis of his collection might be misinterpreted as lack of interest. He asked Eric "Ya? You want to exchange?"

"No *yaar,* I don't collect. I'll get them for you. As a favour, man."

"Ya? What kind do you have?"

"I don't have, man. Come with me to *Patla* and *Jhaaria,* just show me which ones you want. I'll flick them for you."

Jehangir hesitated. Eric put his arm around him: "C'mon man, what you scared for, I'll flick. You just show me and go away." Jehangir pictured the additions to his collection.

He pictured album pages covered with stamps. They went outside, Eric's arms still around him.

Crowds of schoolboys were gathered around the two stalls. A multitude of groping, exploring hands handled the merchandise and browsed absorbedly, a multitude that was a prerequisite for flicking to begin. Jehangir showed Eric the individually wrapped stamps he wanted and moved away. In a few minutes Eric joined him triumphantly.

"Got them?"

"Ya ya. But come inside. He could be watching, man."

Jehangir was thrilled. Eric asked, "You want more or what?"

"Sure," said Jehangir.

"But not today. On Friday. If you do me a favour in visual period on Thursday."

Visual period—with its darkened hall and projector, and the intimacy created by the teacher's policing abilities temporarily suspended. Jehangir's pulse speeded slightly. He remembered Eric's pencil. The cellophane-wrapped stamp packets rustled and crackled in his hand. And there was the promise of more. There had been nothing unpleasant about the pencil. He agreed to Eric's proposal.

On Thursday, the class lined up to go to the Visual Hall. Eric stood behind Jehangir to ensure their seats would be together.

When the room was dark Eric put his hand on Jehangir's thigh and began caressing it. He took Jehangir's hand and placed it on his crotch. It lay there inert. Impatient, he whispered, "Do it, man, c'mon!" But Jehangir's lacklustre stroking was highly unsatisfactory. Eric arrested the hand, reached inside his pants and said, "Okay, hold it tight and rub it like this." He encircled Jehangir's hand with his to show him how. When Jehangir had attained the right pressure and speed he released his own hand to lean back and sigh contentedly. Shortly, Jehangir felt a warm stickiness fill his palm and fingers, and the hardness he held in his hand grew flaccid. Eric shook off the hand. Jehangir wiped his palm with his hanky. Eric borrowed the hanky to wipe himself. "Want me to do it for you?" he asked. But Jehangir declined. He was thinking of his hanky. The odour was interesting, not unpleasant at all, but he would have to find some way of cleaning it before his mother found it.

The following day, Eric presented him with more stamps. Next Thursday's assignation was also set.

And on Sunday Jehangir went to see Dr. Mody at ten o'clock. The wife let him in, muttering something under her breath about being bothered by inconsiderate people on the one day that the family could be together.

Dr. Mody's delight at the new stamps fulfilled Jehangir's every expectation: "Wonderful, wonderful! Where did you get them all? No, no, forget it, don't tell me. You will think I'm trying to learn your tricks. I already have enough stamps to keep me busy in my retirement. Ha! ha!"

After the new stamps had been examined and sorted Dr. Mody said, "Today, as a reward for your enterprise, I'm going to show you a stamp you've never seen before." From the cupboard of biscuit- and sweet-tins he took a small satin-covered box of the type in which rings or bracelets are kept. He opened it and, without removing the stamp from inside, placed it before Jehangir.

The stamp said Espana Correos at the bottom and its denomination was noted in the top left corner: 3 PTAS. The face of the stamp featured a flamenco dancer in the most exquisite detail and colour. But it was something in the woman's countenance, a look, an ineffable sparkle in her eyes, which so captivated Jehangir.

Wordlessly, he studied the stamp. Dr. Mody waited restlessly as the seconds ticked by, then said, "So you like the Spanish dancing-lady. Everyone who sees it likes it. Even my wife who is not interested in stamp-collecting thought it was beautiful. When I retire I can spend more time with the Spanish dancing-lady and all my other stamps." He relaxed once the stamp was locked again in the cupboard.

Jehangir left, trying to imagine the stamp inhabiting the pages of his album, to greet him every time he opened it, with that wonderful sparkle in her eyes. He shut the door behind him and immediately, as if to obliterate his covetous fantasy, loud voices rose up inside the flat. He heard Mrs. Mody's, shrill in argument, and the doctor's, beseeching her not to yell lest the neighbours would hear. Pesi's name was mentioned several times in the quarrel that ensued, and accusations of neglect, and something about the terrible affliction on a son of an unloving father.

When the school week started, Jehangir found himself looking forward to Thursday. His pulse was racing with excitement when visual period came. To save his hanky this time he kept some paper at hand.

Eric did not have to provide much guidance. Jehangir discovered he could control Eric's reactions with variations in speed, pressure and grip. When it was over and Eric offered to do it to him, he did not refuse.

The weeks sped by and Jehangir's collection continued to grow, visual period by visual period. Eric's and his masturbatory partnership was whispered about in class, earning the pair the title of *moothiya-maroo.* He accompanied Eric on the flicking forays, helping to swell the milling crowd and adding to the browsing hands. Then he grew bolder, studied Eric's methods and flicked a few stamps himself.

But this smooth course of stamp-collecting was about to end. *Patla Babu* and *Jhaaria Babu* broke their long tradition of silence and complained to the school. Unlike marbles and *supari,* it was not a question of a few paise a day. When Eric and Jehangir struck, their haul could be totalled in rupees in double digits; the loss was serious enough to make the *Babus* worry about their survival.

The school assigned the case to the head prefect to investigate. He was an ambitious boy, always snooping around, and was also a member of the school debating team and the Road Safety Patrol. Shortly after the complaint was made, he marched into Jehangir's class one afternoon just after lunch break, before the teacher returned, and made what sounded very much like one of his debating speeches: "Two boys in this class have been stealing stamps from *Patla Babu* and *Jhaaria Babu* for the past several weeks. You may ask: who are those boys? No need for names. They know who they are and I know who they are and I am asking them to return the stamps to me tomorrow. There will be no punishment if this is done. The *Babus* just want their stamps back. But if the missing stamps are not returned, the names will be reported to the principal and to the police. It is up to the two boys." Jehangir tried hard to appear normal. He was racked with trepidation, and looked to the unperturbed Eric for guidance. But Eric ignored him. The head prefect left amidst mock applause from the class.

After school, Eric spoke nastily: "You better bring back all the stamps tomorrow." Jehangir, of course, agreed.

There was no trouble with the prefect or the school after the stamps were returned. But Jehangir's stamp collection shrunk pitiably overnight. He slept badly the entire week, worried about explaining to Burjor Uncle the sudden disappearance of the bulk of his collection. His mother assumed the dark rings around his eyes were due to too much reading and not enough fresh air. The thought of stamps or of *Patla Babu* and *Jhaaria Babu* brought an emptiness to his stomach and a bitter taste to his mouth; a general sense of ill-being took possession of him.

He went to see Burjor Uncle on Sunday, leaving behind his stamp album. Mrs. Mody opened the door and turned away silently. She appeared to be in a black rage, which exacerbated Jehangir's own feelings of guilt and shame.

He explained to Burjor Uncle that he had not bothered to bring his album because he had acquired no new stamps since last Sunday, and also, he was not well and would not stay for long.

Dr. Mody was concerned about the boy, so nervous and uneasy; he put it down to his feeling unwell. They looked at some stamps Dr. Mody had received last week. Then Jehangir said he'd better leave.

"But you must see the Spanish dancing-lady before you go. Maybe she will help you feel better. Ha! ha!" And Dr. Mody rose to go to the cupboard for the stamp. Its viewing at the end of each Sunday's session had acquired the significance of an esoteric ritual.

From the next room Mrs. Mody screeched: "Burjorji! Come here at once!" He made a wry face at Jehangir and hurried out.

In the next room, all the vehemence of Mrs. Mody's black rage of that morning poured out upon Dr. Mody: "It has reached the limit now! No time for your own son and Sunday after Sunday sitting with some stranger! What does he have that your own son does not? Are you a *baap* or what? No wonder Pesi has become this way! How can I blame the boy when his own *baap* takes no interest...."

"Shh! The boy is in the next room! Do you want all the neighbours to hear?"

"I don't care! Let them hear! You think they don't know already? You think you are...."

Jehangir's mother next door listened intently. Suddenly, she realized that Jehangir was in there. Listening from one's own house was one thing—hearing a quarrel from inside the quarreller's house was another. It made feigning ignorance very difficult.

She rang the Modys' doorbell and waited, adjusting her *maathabana*. Dr. Mody came to the door.

"Burjorji, forgive me for disturbing your stamping and

collecting work with Jehangir. But I must take him away. Guests have arrived unexpectedly. Jehangir must go to the Irani, we need cold drinks."

"That's okay, he can come next Sunday. He *must* come next Sunday," he added, and noted with satisfaction the frustrated turning away of Mrs. Mody who waited out of sight of the doorway. "Jehangir! Your mother is calling."

Jehangir was relieved at being rescued from the turbulent waters of the Mody household. They left without further conversation, his mother tugging in embarrassment at the knots of her *maathabana*.

As a result of this unfortunate outburst, a period of awkwardness between the women was unavoidable. Mrs. Mody, though far from garrulous, had never let her domestic disappointments interfere with the civilities of neighbourly relations, which she respected and observed at all times. Now for the first time since the arrival of the Modys in Pherozeshah Baag these civilities experienced a hiatus.

When the *muchhiwalla* arrived next morning, instead of striking a joint deal with him as they usually did, Mrs. Mody waited till Mrs. Bulsara had finished. She stationed an eye at her peephole as he emphasized the freshness of his catch. "Look *bai,* it is *saféd paani,"* he said, holding out the pomfret and squeezing it near the gills till white fluid oozed out. When Mrs. Bulsara had paid and gone, Mrs. Mody emerged, while the former took her turn at the peephole. And so it went for a few days till the awkwardness had run its course and things returned to normal.

But not so for Jehangir; on Sunday, he once again had to leave behind his sadly depleted album. To add to his uneasiness, Mrs. Mody invited him in with a greeting of "Come *bawa,* come," and there was something malignant about her smile.

Dr. Mody sat at his desk, shoulders sagging, his hands dangling over the arms of the chair. The desk was bare—not a single stamp anywhere in sight, and the cupboard in the corner locked. The absence of his habitual, comfortable clutter made the room cold and cheerless. He was in low spirits; instead of the crow's-feet at the corners of his eyes were lines of distress and dejection.

"No album again?"

"No. Haven't got any new stamps yet," Jehangir smiled nervously.

Dr. Mody scratched the psoriasis on his elbows. He watched Jehangir carefully as he spoke. "Something very bad has happened to the Spanish dancing-lady stamp. Look," and he displayed the satin-covered box minus its treasure. "It is missing." Half-fearfully, he looked at Jehangir, afraid he would see what he did not want to. But it was inevitable. His last sentence had evoked the head prefect's thundering debating-style speech of a few days ago, and the ugliness of the entire episode revisited Jehangir's features—a final ignominious postscript to Dr. Mody's loss and disillusion.

Dr. Mody shut the box. The boy's reaction, his silence, the absence of his album, confirmed his worse suspicions. More humiliatingly, it seemed his wife was right. With great sadness he rose from his chair. "I have to leave now, something urgent at the College." They parted without a word about next Sunday.

Jehangir never went back. He thought for a few days about the missing stamp and wondered what could have happened to it. Burjor Uncle was too careful to have misplaced it; besides, he never removed it from its special box. And the box was still there. But he did not resent him for concluding he had stolen it. His guilt about *Patla Babu* and *Jhaaria Babu*, about Eric and the stamps was so intense, and the punishment deriving from it so inconsequential, almost non-existent, that he did not mind this undeserved blame. In fact, it served to equilibrate his scales of justice.

His mother questioned him the first few Sundays he stayed home. Feeble excuses about homework, and Burjor Uncle not having new stamps, and it being boring to look at the same stuff every Sunday did not satisfy her. She finally attributed his abnegation of stamps to sensitivity and a regard for the unfortunate state of the Modys' domestic affairs. It pleased her that her son was capable of such concern. She did not press him after that.

4

Pesi was no longer to be seen in Pherozeshah Baag. His absence brought relief to most of the parents at first, and then curiosity. Gradually, it became known that he had been sent away to a boarding-school in Poona.

The boys of the Baag continued to play their games in the compound. For better or worse, the spark was lacking that lent unpredictability to those languid coastal evenings of Bombay; evenings that could so easily trap the unwary, adult or child, within a circle of lassitude and depression in which time hung heavy and suffocating.

Jehangir no longer sat on the stone steps of C Block in the evenings. He found it difficult to confront Dr. Mody day after day. Besides, the boys he used to watch at play suspected some kind of connection between Pesi's being sent away to boarding-school, Jehangir's former friendship with Dr. Mody and the emerging of Dr. Mody's constant sorrow and despair (which he had tried so hard to keep private all along, and succeeded, but was now visible for all to see). And the boys resented Jehangir for whatever his part in it was; they bore him open antagonism.

Dr. Mody was no more the jovial figure the boys had grown to love and respect. When his car turned into the compound in the evenings, he still waved, but no crow's-feet appeared at his eyes, no smile, no jokes.

Two years passed since the Mody family's arrival in Pherozeshah Baag.

In school, Jehangir was as isolated as in the Baag. Most of his effeminateness had, of late, transformed into vigorous signs of impending manhood. Eric D'Souza had been expelled for attempting to sodomize a junior boy. Jehangir had not been involved in this affair, but most of his classmates related it to the furtive activities of their callow days and the stamp-flicking. *Patla Babu* and *Jhaaria Babu* had disappeared from the pavement outside St. Xavier's. The Bombay police, in a misinterpretation of the nation's mandate—*garibi hatao* (eradicate poverty)—conducted periodic round-ups of pavement dwellers, sweeping into their vans beggars and street-vendors, cripples and alcoholics, the homeless and the hungry, and dumped them somewhere outside the city limits; when the human detritus made its way back into the city another clean-up was scheduled. *Patla Babu* and *Jhaaria Babu* were snared in one of these raids, and never found their way back. Eyewitnesses said their stalls were smashed up and *Patla Babu* received a *lathi* across his forehead for trying to salvage some of his inventory. They were not seen again.

Two years passed since Jehangir's visits to Dr. Mody had ceased.

It was getting close to the time for another transfer for Dr. Mody. When the inevitable orders were received, he went to Ahmedabad to make arrangements. Mrs. Mody was to join her husband after a few days. Pesi was still in boarding-school, and would stay there.

So when news arrived from Ahmedabad of Dr. Mody's death of heart failure, Mrs. Mody was alone in the flat. She went next door with the telegram and broke down.

The Bulsaras helped with all the arrangements. The body was brought to Bombay by car for a proper Parsee funeral.

Pesi came from Poona for the funeral, then went back to boarding-school.

The events were talked about for days afterwards, the stories spreading first in C Block, then through A and B. Commiseration for Mrs. Mody was general. The ordeal of the body during the two-day car journey from Ahmedabad was particularly horrifying and was discussed endlessly. Embalming was not allowed according to Parsee rituals, and the body in the trunk, although packed with ice, had started to smell horribly in the heat of the Deccan Plateau, which the car had had to traverse. Poor Dr. Mody, they said, who never went a day without a bath and talcum powder in life, to undergo this in death. Someone even had, on good authority, a count of the number of eau de cologne bottles used by Mrs. Mody and the three occupants of the car during the journey—it was the only way they could draw a breath, through cologne-watered handkerchiefs. And it was also said that ever after, these four could never use eau de cologne—opening a bottle was like opening the car trunk with Dr. Mody's decomposing corpse.

A year after the funeral, Mrs. Mody was still living in Pherozeshah Baag. Time and grief had softened her looks, and she was no longer the harsh and dour-faced woman Jehangir had seen during his first Sunday visit. She had decided to make the flat her permanent home now, and the trustees of the Baag granted her request "in view of the unfortunate circumstances." There were some protests about this, particularly from those whose sons or daughters had been postponing marriages and families till flats became available. But the majority, in respect of Dr. Mody's memory, agreed with the trustees' decision. Pesi continued to attend boarding-school.

One day, shortly after her application had been approved by the trustees, Mrs. Mody visited Mrs. Bulsara. They sat and talked of old times, when they had first moved in, and the disagreements she had had with her husband over Pesi and Pesi's future; tears came to her eyes, and also to Mrs. Bulsara's, who tugged at a corner of her *maathabana* to reach it to her eyes and dry them. Mrs. Mody confessed how she had hated Jehangir's Sunday visits although he was such a fine boy, because she was worried about the way poor Burjorji was neglecting Pesi: "But he could not help it. That was the way he was. Sometimes he would wish *Khoedai* had given him a daughter instead of a son. Pesi disappointed him in everything, in all his plans, and..." and here she burst into uncontrollable sobs.

Finally, after her tears subsided, she asked, "Is Jehangir home?" He wasn't. "Would you ask him to come and see me this Sunday? At ten? Tell him I won't keep him long."

Jehangir was a bit apprehensive when his mother gave him the message. He couldn't imagine why Mrs. Mody would want to see him.

On Sunday, as he prepared to go next door, he was reminded of the Sundays with Dr. Mody, the kindly man who had befriended him, opened up a new world for him, and then repudiated him for something he had not done. He remembered the way he would scratch the greyish-red patches of psoriasis on his elbows. He could still picture the sorrow on his face as, with the utmost reluctance, he had made his decision to end the friendship. Jehangir had not blamed Dr. Mody then, and he still did not; he knew how overwhelmingly the evidence had been against him, and how much that stamp had meant to Dr. Mody.

Mrs. Mody led him in by his arm: "Will you drink something?"

"No, thank you."

"Not feeling shy, are you? You always were shy." She asked him about school, and which college he would go to next year. She told him a little about Pesi, who was still in boarding-school and had repeated his final year twice. She sighed. "I asked you to come today because there is something I wanted to give you. Something of Burjor Uncle's. I thought about it for many days. Pesi is not interested, and I don't know anything about it. Will you take his collection?"

"The album in his drawer?" asked Jehangir, a little surprised.

"Everything. The album, all the boxes, everything in the cupboard. I know you will use it well. Burjor would have done the same."

Jehangir was speechless. He had stopped collecting stamps, and they no longer held the fascination they once did. Nonetheless, he was familiar with the size of the collection, and the sheer magnitude of what he was now being offered had its effect. He remembered the awe with which he had looked inside the cupboard the first time its doors had been opened before him. So many sweet-tins, cardboard boxes, biscuit tins....

"You will take it? As a favour to me, yes?" she asked a second time, and Jehangir nodded. "You have some time today? Whenever you like, just take it." He said he would ask his mother and come back.

There was a huge, old iron trunk that lay under Jehangir's bed. It was dented in several places and the lid would not shut properly. Undisturbed for years, it had rusted peacefully beneath the bed. His mother agreed that the rags it held could be thrown away and the stamps temporarily stored in it till Jehangir organized them into albums. He emptied the trunk, wiped it out, lined it with brown paper and went next door to bring back the stamps.

Several trips later, Dr. Mody's cupboard stood empty. Jehangir looked around the room in which he had once spent so many happy hours. The desk was in exactly the same position, and the two chairs. He turned to go, almost forgetting, and went back to the desk. Yes, there it was in the drawer, Dr. Mody's first album, given him by his

Nusserwanji Uncle. He started to turn the heavily laden pages. They rustled in a peculiar way—what was it about that sound? Then he remembered: that first Sunday, and he could almost hear Dr. Mody again, the soft inspired tones speaking of promises and dreams, quite different from his usual booming, jovial voice, and that faraway look in his eyes, which had once glinted with rage when Pesi had tried to bully him....

Mrs. Mody came into the room. He shut the album, startled: "This is the last lot." He stopped to thank her but she interrupted: "No, no. What is the thank you for? You are doing favour to me by taking it, you are helping me to do what Burjor would like." She took his arm. "I wanted to tell you. From the collection one stamp is missing. With the picture of the dancing-lady."

"I know!" said Jehangir. "That's the one Burjor Uncle lost and thought that I...."

Mrs. Mody squeezed his arm, which she was still holding, and he fell silent. She spoke softly, but without guilt: "He did not lose it. I destroyed it." Then her eyes went moist as she watched the disbelief on his face. She wanted to say more, to explain, but could not, and clung to his arm. Finally, her voice quavering pitiably, she managed to say, "Forgive an old lady," and patted his cheek. Jehangir left in silence, suddenly feeling very ashamed.

Over the next few days, he tried to impose some order on that greatly chaotic mass of stamps. He was hoping that sooner or later his interest in philately would be rekindled. But that did not happen; the task remained futile and dry and boring. The meaningless squares of paper refused to come to life as they used to in Dr. Mody's room every Sunday at ten o'clock. Jehangir shut the trunk and pushed it back under his bed where it had lain untroubled for so many years.

From time to time his mother reminded him about the

stamps: "Do something Jehangoo, do something with them." He said he would when he felt like it and had the time; he wasn't interested for now.

After several months, Jehangir pulled out the trunk again. The night before, his sleep had been disturbed by a faint and peculiar rustling sound seeming to come from inside the trunk.

The lid was thrown back to reveal clusters of cockroaches. They tried to scuttle to safety, and Jehangir killed a few with his slipper. Some ran under the bed into hard-to-reach corners; others sought out the trunk's deeper recesses.

A cursory examination showed that besides cockroaches, the trunk was also infested with white ants. All the albums had been ravaged. Jehangir picked one up and, as the pages started to fall to pieces in his hand, remembered what Dr. Mody used to say: "This is my retirement hobby. I will spend my retirement with my stamps."

Most of the stamps that had not been destroyed outright were damaged in one way or another. They bore haphazard perforations and brown stains of the type associated with insects and household pests. It was doubtful if anything of value remained in the trunk.

Lesley Krueger

Exiles

It was tea-time at my grandmother's farm. There were hot triangular scones made in the fry-pan and smelling like wool, flour, heaven. Slices of dark drenched fruitcake, dusty with powdered sugar. Buttery shortbread with fork prints on top, cinnamon-crusted teacake, little crustless sandwiches that were meagre as gentility: my grandmother let us know she came from better, although that did not mean we did. She was one of the wave of Scots immigrants who came to Canada after the First World War. Most of them got skilled jobs in the cities, but my grandfather brought her to this isolated dairy farm. Maybe she would have been happier in the city, although I grew to think she was the type to feel vindicated by misery. She was a tall, flat woman, who sat behind her foldaway cardboard tea-table like an Edwardian lady; polished her silver every three weeks; put doilies on the cake plates: probably repeating the arrangements of a table she had once admired. Not, I think, her parents'. We drove there every Sunday. My father was from South Africa himself, but he too was like many exiles in having no curiosity about his new country. We never travelled anywhere else.

I got to ride in the front seat beside him. My father always kept the plastic factory covers on the seats, and when it was a hot day the bare part of my legs sweated and sucked against them. Sometimes I tried to make disgusting kissy noises. "Stop that, Alison," my father said. Stup thet, Elison. He spoke with an accent as flat as the slap of his hand: an older father, rather stiff; one of those redheads who had just faded and dried up, so the freckles seemed caught in the lines around his eyes like stepped-on confetti. But he was doting, if not affectionate. His weakness was for children, for me in particular. That was how he put it. His strength, as he also put it, was in his convictions. He had left South Africa after his first wife died and he found he could no longer stomach the colour bar. Yet I have come to understand that my father was one of those people who see past the everyday to a great and demanding truth, then just keep seeing past the everyday. He left the country, but he still expected an easy, served life. He treated my mother like a kaffir.

She was a fat woman. In our suburb, there were mothers from the city and mothers from the farm, and the farm women still wore faded house dresses in dated styles put on to declare they were older. My mother's favourite was a blue dress with white piping. She would stretch up to hang out the laundry and cry happily, "Watch me, I'll bust my buttons." She never did get into the citified habit of dieting, which seemed to go on in a different world, where being thin might get you something. These women were married, they had got what they wanted, and despite what I have come to feel it is anachronistic to think them mistaken. At the same time, the woman next door to us wore pedal-pushers and had affairs: the fifties were not really in lockstep, there was this layering of eras, especially when there were immigrants in the neighbourhood, whether from other countries or from farms. But I wanted painfully for my mother to be modern: if she went into better stores, she might know which clothes to buy for me. She would hold up some misshapen bag of a sailor dress with a cheap vinyl belt. "Pretty." I raged at her; she liked my brother best. On our drives, she sat with him in the back seat and sang songs from movie musicals. *The King and I. Carousel.* Her voice was sweet and rather breathless.

Sometimes I try to imagine the first drive my father took to my grandmother's farm. My mother had just graduated from high school, he was 44 and had an introduction to the family from their relatives in South Africa. It must have seemed a desolate trip as he picked his way into the Interior. My grandmother had the last farm, the end-of-the-world farm, cut right up the base of the foothills so the final, crossed-log fence held back the forest, or tried to; the growth was so wild, the salal and bracken, that it seemed to roll down the hills, while the mist tumbled on top of it like a loose and ghostly avalanche. The house was nearly empty too. My grandmother's husband had died long before and the children were all grown up, even though my grandmother was not much older than my father. My mother was the last one left at home. I see her opening the door: ripe, shy, blooming. She was already heavy, but she had heavier hair that bowed her neck like a rose blown open. Extraordinary skin, a merry smile: that is what the pictures show, although I always wondered why my father married her and not my grandmother.

"Well Mrs. Burns," my father would ask. "And tell me about the cattle. Are you breeding calves yet with the front legs shorter, so they can graze uphill?"

"You forget, Mr. MacIntyre, they have to get back down."

Practised jokes, all of them. I step back, and from one angle I see these formal people going through their tea in a routine that is a parody of graciousness. I see myself as a big, dark, secretive child, who watched them and—the week I am thinking of—turned them upside down. From another angle, I see only that the excessive order of the parlour and the meal was common among women immigrants. My grandmother controlled what she could control. It must have been difficult. She left Scotland only because her husband decided they should go. She was pregnant, she had no choice; I wonder if he waited until then. I also wonder if the word for women like my grandmother was immigrant, or if it was really exile. From what I have seen since, exile does not mean simply that you cannot go back. Sometimes it is also that you cannot go.

I am thinking of Arnaud, a man of complicated background. His parents were Lebanese, but he was brought up around West Africa. Dakar, Ouagadougou: he rolled out the names like funky drum beats, slightly mocking and syncopated. He had a trader's closed face, and wall eyes that made him look like he was watching the fall of two diverging stars. We met at university, he asked me out, and I think it was his slight deformity that made me accept, to prove I was above caring about it. But the truth was, I wouldn't have gone out with Arnaud if I hadn't had something to prove, and by the end of the evening it was clear I never would again; I could not even sleep with him that night in compensation. We were at a coffee house. It was very small and dim; a folksinger walked on stage. In the corner I saw an elegant man in a fisherman's knit sweater who looked a little bit like Lenin. Between sets, Arnaud and I talked about Casablanca: in his case the city, in mine the movie. I confessed I wanted to be as impeccably beautiful as Ingrid Bergman. Since I had turned out large this must have sounded pathetic. But I suppose I wanted to make myself seem pathetic, so he would not want to go out with me again either. It didn't register though, he talked about his home. He said he could never go back because the conditions would seem too primitive.

"My family are thieves," he told me. "Thieves. Which is to say merchants, in West Africa it is the same thing. Another word might be gamblers. You cannot imagine the gambling fever there is in Senegal. I had a guitar I liked very much, but sometimes my father would come for my guitar, having lost even that. Now I have a suite free gratis at the Caesar's Palace gambling casino in Las Vegas for one week, once a year, because I have introduced to them the West African Lebanese merchant gamblers. You don't believe me?"

I did not.

"How can you believe me? You do not know what I have seen. In Senegal every year the fishermen sacrifice a baby to the sea. It is true. The missionaries think they have stopped it but they have not. I will tell you, in another place an army marched out of the bush to try to overthrow the government. One thousand men. Bang, bang, there is shooting, some killed, not all. But they all disappeared. I would like you to tell me where they went. Eaten. They were all eaten by the villagers. It is true. I have seen barbecues, piglets I think, until I look closer and see the heads of babies lined up along the fence. This also, unfortunately, is true."

It was a subtle revenge. I felt deeply ignorant, because I did not know when to stop believing him. The casino? The fishermen? The coup? Arnaud made me feel like a foolish child, who had been spoiled and over-protected. Yet my parents had not spoiled me, and my mother in particular offered little protection. I decided Arnaud must be a liar, and by the end of the evening I believed nothing that he said. Then we were saying goodbye. I was dropping him off in my beat-up old car and hoping he would get out quickly. There was a pause though as he fumbled for the handle in the dark. Then he had it, but instead of opening the door immediately he turned and took my hand. I held my breath. "Still," he said in a kind voice, "there is something in you of Ingrid Bergman."

There were crumbly butter tarts, if my mother had brought them. Or her angel-food cake, with its field of sugar sparkles on the icing. I liked to have tea at my grandmother's farm, as long as no-one compared me to my mother. We both liked to eat. But while she worked her way steadily and happily through half a pan of teacake, I snatched shortbread off the plate, gobbled it down and sat with my feet swinging off the floor like an innocent.

"Sit still, Alison," my father would say.

"I want to go outside."

There were kittens, calves; often I had plans. The week I am thinking of, I had a plan.

"What do you say then?"

"Please."

This plan concerned the weedy logging road that ran through the hills behind the farm. On one of these hills, a fresh spring stream ran out of the bush and along the road, cutting a red and rocky channel through the dirt to the base of the hill, where it sniggled off again. I planned to divert this stream partway down the hill by angling a channel across the road, so the stream dropped off its edge like a waterfall. I thought it was a lovely thing, to make a waterfall.

"Go on, then." I hopped off the couch. But I had not gone far when I saw that my mother had hopped up too.

"I think I'll just go get some air with the children." She must have felt dessicated by her mother's conversation. She liked to talk with her friends about movie stars and royalty. The Queen may be Queen, she said shrewdly, but Philip no doubt rules the roost. Yet I felt no sympathy for my mother. She made us get our coats, when I had particularly planned to forget my coat, and make my brother forget his. Davey figured in my plan. He was the crew.

"Let's just go for a nice walk."

"I don't want to go for any walk," I mumbled.

"What, Alison?" she asked. Then, in a Mother voice, "What's the matter, Alison?"

"I want to go and play."

"Hide and seek," Davey giggled.

"Alison," my father warned. The pedal-pusher mothers were friends with their girls. They wore the same clothes in the daytime and were ravishingly soignee at night in a way that was as much a promise to their daughters as their husbands. Mine did not court me, she made no secret of the fact that Davey was her favourite. I usually accepted this in a matter-of-fact way that reassures me now, when I look at my own daughter and think about children surviving their parents. Yet sometimes it also frightened me to think that she might resent me as much as I resented her. I wanted to feel you got better as you got older; I wanted this security. Security was a big word in the fifties, and it often got confused in this way with predictability and progress. We thought that things got better and better: in the end we would all own houses with swimming-pools. Yet my mother's resentment made me feel thoroughly insecure. She made me feel ashamed and dirty. For some reason I got a mental picture of myself as someone very small, with a big head and two enormous front teeth. That ugly. Such a monstrous and unlovable daughter.

"Sure," I said humbly. "Hide and seek." My mother liked this better than a walk. She liked to sit and watch us play. But suddenly I had a brainstorm, and my shame did its hot trick of turning back into resentment. I found myself dancing and pointing brightly at my mother.

"You're It. You're It." It was a weird dance of feverish falseness. I felt sick, and it came out as excitement. "You be It. Please?"

"Oh, really," my mother said, and looked down at her high-heeled shoes.

"Please?" Davey asked, catching the excitement. He joined me in a dance on his babyish-fat legs. Tree trunks, she called them, kneeding them as he sat sometimes, even now, on her soft and spreading lap. She smiled down at his wriggling. Then suddenly shook her thick hair back like a wilful child.

"Hide and seek," she said, in an exhilarated, defiant voice, before covering her mouth wide with one hand to hide her horrified giggle. But she had done it. Davey pulled her toward the centre of the farmyard while I trailed behind them, maliciously surprised that she could be so stupid. Her fat bottom lapped ahead of me: imagine her nerve. She was suddenly like the mothers who wore clothes that were too young for them. Barettes in their hair, little circle skirts for skating. They wanted to use the fathers, to be lazy, to get out of things: we saw this. I see now that my mother was ashamed of herself, but that she wanted to use this occasion, in a confused way, to break a mould. So we would close our eyes and count to fifty while she hid, then we would run to find her. Davey giggled happily at the game, and plastered his hands across his face. I made a show of doing the same, so for a moment I felt my humid breath heat my cold nose and screaming teeth. It was April and chilly. But when I felt my mother turn to leave, I peeked, and while I counted out I watched her mince between the ruts and the cowpats: in the wide barn door.

"Fifty," I said, so Davey pulled his hands down and blinked in the sun. He looked around, then started a blind-little-boy walk into the equipment shed, where he squatted down, and peered solemnly beneath a tractor. I let him lead. But I was three years older and I could tend him toward the barn, without his suspecting. I had no concrete plan. It was just that cheating once made it likely I would cheat again. The possibilities lay strewn around the farmyard like bright, half-hidden Easter eggs. We went into the barn, out of the chill. I only shivered harder.

The cattle were out to pasture, but the scrawny, shrieking cats were down. Davey stooped to pat one, then ran off in a scalloping line, looking into each stall individually. I stayed near the door, scrubbing a cat's ears as my excuse, but really listening for my mother. Then I heard her giggle in the hay-loft.

"Here!" I called to Davey. I ran toward the hayloft, remembering as I did so that the ladder stood loose against the ceiling. A plan gathered with the saliva in my mouth, so

I tasted salt and temptation. Davey meanwhile pumped toward me, laughing, and we met at the foot of the ladder. "I know you're up there," I called triumphantly. "I *know.*" Then I yanked the ladder down and trapped her.

"Don't," Davey cried.

"I did it," I yelled. Then I heard a scuffling overhead like cats and mice, and my mother leaned out of the hole so her cheeks were hanging.

"You put that back, Alison," she said. She spoke in a Mother voice, but an eighth too fast. She was scared; I treasured that. "You do what I tell you," she warned.

"No," I sauced. I was not sure what I would do. I was not even sure I could lift the ladder back. Davey couldn't.

"Oh, put it back Alison, please." The weak, exhaled coaxing. She was so permanently convinced, no matter what happened, that she was to blame. It made me want to gut her.

"No," I howled, and ran splay-footed out of the barn. Hate lifted me over the fields, the fence, up the ragged logging road. I was not ordinarily much of a runner, but that day I found it in me to hurl, tasting more and more the saliva salt, feeling my sides stitch, my socks fall. I reached my stream and straddled it: I was that big and it was so small. In fact I had just one problem in the world. I needed a tool to dig my channel, and channel my waterfall over the road. A wooden tool, a sharpened stick. I deeked into the woods to find one.

In the spring, toadstools grew on fallen logs, thick as words. There were little white ones with conical caps, tiny orange ones with fluted gills. Table fungus grew like ledges on fallen, crumbling trees. I squatted over them, then found I had to pee and let my panties drop right there, until a thick, rotting pong seemed to rise around me. Soon afterward I found my stick, and headed back to gouge my channel. It was messy work. I started at the edge of the road, planning to work backwards, so the last dig would let the water cascade into my completed channel. It was hard; the dirt made half-moons under my nails. Yet I went on, thinking of my waterfall bounding off the road like a white dog loose and running. It is an absolute fact that I forgot all about my mother.

After university, when I was absorbing pop psychology, I thought I fought with my mother because I was too much like her. I saw things in physical terms, and it is true I have her tendency to put on weight. But it is also not true in a hundred other ways, or only almost true: I sometimes wonder now how psychologists can say the approximate things they do with such conviction. I did not wonder then though. In my mid-twenties, I was both vulnerable to firm people and attracted to them. The psychologists, the political visionaries, Mustapha: I do not speak in merely sexual terms.

Mustapha was a delegate in our city from the South African guerrillas. I worked with him trying to convince companies to divest themselves of their South African interests. His background was Moslem East Indian, but his family had lived for several generations on the Cape. He was a bony man, with long wrists extending fom his polyester safari suits, and an evangelical turn, although he was saved from being didactic by a wicked sense of humour. He would like to have thought women are equal, but his background worked against him: there was a suggestion of forebearance about him, a suggestion of contempt. He used to cook me dinner sometimes, but it cost him. He huddled over the hotplate in his monkish little apartment and hectored the vegetables on their limpness, their toughness, their outrageous capitalistic price. Of course I caught the undertone, and it unsettled me. It made me question my worth; exiles always do this; Mustapha, Arnaud. They imply they are of international importance, while your interest is merely regional. But I am no saint, I did fight back. I nagged him about his insistence on saying "racist" before "South Africa," since I found it not only redundant but inelegant.

"The truth does not wear white gloves and drink tea," Mustapha said ferociously. He made this show of loving the truth. Yet, he wore a toupee. An awful toupee, cheap and plastic. More than that: a toupee for a white man, with a white scalp and part, while Mustapha was quite dark. When you looked at it, you couldn't help wondering in what other ways he was fooling himself, or trying to fool other people. One night over beer and curry I got drunk enough to challenge him on it.

"Alas," he sighed theatrically, and lifted off the toupee as if it were a crown. "I tried one day to darken his scalp with shoe dye, Nut Brown, but in the rain it ran down over my face in big black tears. I must tell you, even I found that too obvious a piece of hyperbole. I scrubbed him clean, and decided if I am to wear a toupee, it must announce itself to the world as a toupee." He put it back on. "Preferring plain truths," he said, and cracked up laughing.

Exiles. At first I did not really notice that I was surrounded by them. My father and grandmother were merely there, and only exotic when I wanted to make them appear so on the playground. Children seem to feel this conflict, especially suburban children of such uniform background and class. We want to belong, while seeming special; to be what everyone else is and more. Yet I could never get the proportions right. I was usually so large that I was a walking parody of this suburban ideal, and I never really felt at ease in any group of people. Only outdoors did I feel proportionate. Scratching out my ridiculous channel that day in the hills beyond my grandmother's farm I felt worthy, competent and grand. It was a lovely day. The cedars, firs, the bushy salal all looked dewy and crystal in the clear mountain air. Each one looked separate; they stood out just like me.

This did not last. The stick soon broke. My hands got sore. The wind blew up, it was time to go. But as I started back, even though my channel was just a scratch in the road, I was happy and planned to finish it next Sunday. It did not occur to me that I might not be allowed. My coat hung wrecked, my socks bled mud. And of course there was the barn. I remembered that when I kneed up the fence and saw it laid down in the farmyard below me. Red, unavoidable. I remembered it all and got horror splashing in my head like water. Once before something like this happened, when my mother had made me turn off the television during a thunderstorm. The next day I pulled her laundry from the line and threw it around the yard, while the retarded girl who lived next door cried, "Pretty, pretty." Now I saw that I had done it again, and started running in confusion. Running, stumbling down the pasture, so the sandy grit chafed behind my knees. I checked the barn; it was empty. Checked the kitchen, and of course they were waiting.

Davey sat drinking milk at the table. I saw him first, and when he saw me he slipped down and left the kitchen like a cat uncurling. Behind him was my mother. I saw that she had placed herself so I would have to face her when I came in. She had also adjusted her expression, so it was sorrowful and accusing. I knew she had adjusted it; left to herself, she would just whine. But my grandmother stood behind her.

"Look at the child," my grandmother cried. I turned to close the mudroom door, because I was going to smile. Of course I was; I felt victorious. Before I saw my mother, after episodes like this, I was ready to be wrong. When I did see her, I thought that she deserved it.

"Well missy?" my father asked. I turned to see that he was standing in a dim angle of the kitchen, beside the subtly gleaming wood stove. He seemed calm, but I knew that he was furious. I knew what was coming, and did not care. I did not care.

"Look at your coat," Grandmother scolded. "Look what you've done to your mother." I looked, and smirked. She saw this; my mother was subtle and quick in sensing what others think of her, although she was also quick to believe them. In this lay the reason she had always submitted; also her generosity. She shuddered now, and hiccoughed a sob, so my grandmother let her hand fall onto her shoulder. This is the only time I ever saw my grandmother caress anyone.

"Well missy?" my father warned. I could not control my nonchalance.

"I forgot."

"She forgot *me.*" my mother cried. There was a long pause, during which I did not apologize. Then I felt proud of myself and giggled. My grandmother made a disgusted sound.

"She deserves a whipping." Then she put her hand on my mother's shoulder as if to balance herself. I saw all this as sharp as winter. Cutting, clear. I saw the kitchen was nothing but different permutations of anger. Even the stove seemed furiously polished, the white sink shrilly clean. I saw my father step toward the centre of the room and look at my mother, although it was my grandmother who had spoken. I saw my mother pout insistently until he looked down. He looked down, and I could not see what he was thinking. But with his head lowered, he undid his brown leather belt and held it loosely, so its buckle dragged on the floor. Then suddenly he lunged, and harder than before or since he grabbed my shoulder and flung me around, so my hands were on a chair back and my bottom was bent toward him. He flung back my coat. Flung back my shirt, baring dirty underpants. And more quickly than possible he brought his belt down so I cried as it whipped ice against my buttocks. There was a pause, during which my mother breathed.

"Oh." Breathed impersonally, as if someone had asked her for directions that she could not give.

"Count them out," my father said. "That was one."

"One," I yelped. I tried to stand outside myself, and to float far, far above them. I wanted to look down on my furious and parched-looking father; my mother, who jumped reflexively each time he hit, my mischievous and spiteful grandmother. What was she doing here? This occurred to me suddenly. What was she doing on this solitary farm at the edge of the world? She, who as her only hobby played at being a lady. It is true, and probably just as well, that children do not usually see the singularity of their family lives. They accept what is there, they do not see alternatives. But that day I suddenly realized that my grandmother did not have to live as she did. She could leave. I could leave. My father hit me.

"No," I cried, and lunged away. My father quickly grabbed me by the coat and brought his belt down with his free hand.

"Oh," my mother breathed again, although this time it was as if she were waking.

"You leave me alone," I cried, balking, angry. Sprawling. As I fell, my father kneeled with one knee on my back to pin me to the floor. It is curious, he grunted but said nothing. My mother was the one who spoke.

"It's really too bad," I looked up to see that my grandmother still had her hands on my mother's shoulders, although now it was to try to keep her down. She failed; my mother shook her off impatiently and stood. You would think a normally timid and breathless younger daughter would be scared of this mother, but in fact she always seemed lazy and negligent at the farm, as if she had something to hold over my grandmother. My father, I suppose. Who struck me.

"Don't!" I cried.

"Count them out."

"*I will not.*"

"That's five," my mother told him nervously. "Really, don't you think it's enough?" He hit me. I thrashed, but he had me pinned to the floor.

"Isn't that enough?" my mother asked. "That's enough, isn't it?" He hit me again. "I think that's—"

"Mrs. MacIntyre," my father said fiercely. "If you would *make up your mind* for once in your life." Then he lashed me harshly. My mother made a soft sound. She took two steps forward, and in her face I saw defiance. Then retreat. I saw her retreat and let my head sink back onto the floor. I shook uncontrollably now. The toes of my shoes rattled on the linoleum. Then I heard the buckle drop, and felt warm leather curl across my legs. I exhaled gladly.

"Ach," my father spit. Then suddenly he swung and slapped me with the flat of his hand, so my loosened buttocks reverberated. I felt betrayed, but it was my mother's cry that lingered. It was a surprised and surprising sound, as if he had hit her instead of me. Then she sobbed in, making us all turn toward her. My father's voice was scornful.

"Why do you let this happen?" he asked, and stared at her a long time. Then he turned to my grandmother. "Why did you let this happen?" he repeated, with the pinpricking subtlety—what?—of the disappointed husband or the disappointed lover? I scrambled up, I could not tell. But I can taste and feel his voice even now, underneath my breastbone: it is that deep, that dark, that tender. When I wonder, now, why my father left South Africa instead of staying to fight for his beliefs, it is this sound I remember, for in it was a distant acknowledgement of my wrong, his difficult feelings for my grandmother and his contempt for my mother, whom he said let that happen. I think I understand it then.

I could have travelled many routes from that first rebellion. I might have fought for native rights, for the environment, for unions. Certainly I am a feminist. Yet I have worked mainly for the causes of exiles. I suppose I felt I belonged with them, in a community of displaced souls. I have always been so out-of-step: overweight in an era of thin women; motherly, but blessed with just one child; a feminist who counted the miles in protest marches as exercise in her beauty magazine diets. What I didn't see for a long time however is that exiles belong very fervently and exclusively to an idea, even if it is only an idea of themselves, as is the case with poor Arnaud. But last year I joined the Catholic Church when I married a man who had been brought up Catholic. Both Rick and I are activists, and share a somehow suburban sense of responsibility. I am the impatient one, and forever rebellious; Rick is methodical and rather enjoys his high and benign place in the various movements for social change. But he is not evangelical, the conversion was not his idea; nor was it the grateful female surrender one friend charged. In fact I think of it as an active and characteristically vigorous embrace. But it did not occur to me that it might also be called exile, until I saw the reaction of my family. Then I understood that implicit in the idea of following is that you must leave.

I told them at the farm on Sunday afternoon. My grandmother still ran it with her hired hands, and I had come to admire what I saw as her decision to be strong when she could have given in, moved to town, become a mere lady. Surely she could have sold the place. Or maybe not, maybe she had to keep it until one of my shrewder cousins took a look at the unemployment rate this year and decided to become a farmer. Maybe she just lacked the will to uproot a second time, but in the days just before my marriage I was inclined to grant everyone energy, principles and purpose, since I thought these were the component parts of happiness, and I hoped everyone else was happy too.

I drove out alone, passing my parents at one point in the Valley. Latterly my mother drove—slowly and persistently—while my father nagged her and read out every road sign. He had become a talkative old man. But an old man: I was shocked one day, when he opened the screen door, to see that his hands had gone spotted, and his fingers dwindled toward a faint tinge of purple at the ends. My mother however was still at the blowy end of her prime. Her complexion had remained good, with a fat woman's healthy and impermeable gleam. She was still jolly, but shrewd lately too, and she had begun to show a talent for malice that sometimes puzzled me. Maybe she had finally picked it up from her mother. Sometimes I am afraid that I have too.

The slices of fruitcake were smaller now. There were fingers of cheddar cheese served with celery and crackers that no-one bothered to call biscuits. It was over this inattentive tea that I made my announcement. I did a bad job, speaking bluntly when I should have been circuitous: my grandmother was a Protestant from the days when that meant looking down on Catholics. There was a long silence.

"Good for you," my mother said finally. When I looked over, I saw that she had not spoken earlier simply because her mouth was full of cake. "Trust Alison to do what no-one else would."

"Thank you," I said. I saw that the other two were silent out of a deep bitterness, which worked at the corners of their mouths. My grandmother took a sip of tea and put her cup back precisely in its saucer.

"I suppose you're going to whelp each year now until you're forty," she said. "I thought we'd gone beyond that." She had never liked me. *Clumsy child,* she always cried. *Hopeless child.* She was about the same age as Davey. It dawned on me now that she had none of my father's fondness for children. As well that he had never noticed. Children must have been a sexual reminder to her, or perhaps merely wicked in themselves. Davey and I had intruded into her house; she thought we were a bad smell. Yet it did not occur to me to pity her.

"I would never have thought of you as vulgar," I said. My father spoke up fiercely.

"You're not to speak to your grandmother that way. What she says is right. After all your talk, where will you be? Barefoot, pregnant and in the kitchen."

I laughed angrily. But from my mother's chair, there came another sound. She levered herself up, with elbows and grunts and a chuckle. There was a curious sensuousness in her unrepentant roll. I was reminded of someone turning over in bed.

"Oh I don't know," she told my father. "I seem to remember, you wanted children bad enough yourself."

It was after this I first began to think of my father's first visits to the farm. He has described South Africa to me as a golden country, so coming to our dark and tangled Coast must have thoroughly disheartened him. He could not love it. Exile is a pragmatic and intellectual decision. Your emotions remain with the homeland and you bring not love, but merely a strong capacity for nostalgia. Surely that is true of me as well, and it is perhaps why converts are so notoriously stringent: the rigorous mind is engaged, and there is little softening from emotion. How comforting for my father, then, to reach my grandmother's farm and find my mother waiting there. Pink, young and compliant: he always spoke of his weakness for children, which I saw now as simply the most potent form taken by nostalgia.

"And look what it's got me," he said bitterly, in answer to my mother. His shrug included her as well as me. He sat across from us with his knees tight, his lips tight, his chin dancing in a febrile quiver. I found it ghastly to see someone regret all the pleasure in his life this way.

"They're good kids," my mother answered complacently. She planted a patronizing smile on my grandmother and took another bite of her cake. "This one was a stubborn donkey, but neither of them ever gave me much trouble. I could have had ten myself." My grandmother sipped her tea, and once more put her cup back in its saucer.

"I think we'll have rain," she told my father. And that was all they ever said.

Ban Mai

Upstream the bamboo suspension bridge lilted like a bright Thai song as the monk walked delicately across it. He was dressed in saffron. Women were forbidden to touch him, but I did as much by staring at his cool bare brown head and long, intertwined fingers. A few weeks before this, when I was riding a freak bus through Nepal, I had been very sick until another monk leaned across the aisle and looked directly in my eyes. I fell asleep immediately and woke up feeling better. He made me believe in the power of monks here, and their kindliness, and what is more friends at home believed me when I told my story, although they would have been embarrassed if I had been talking about one of the TV faith healers we get in the West. The East is often just as tacky, but the rituals there can also seem as casual and off-hand as the manners of a gentleman, which we admire for their grace. In our boat, below the monk's bridge, the hill tribe women who sat across from me put a purple orchid in the water just before we pushed off, and I could not tell if she was making an offering for a safe journey, or if she had simply discarded it.

The passenger boats that ran up and down the river here were really no more than long outboards, with room for maybe twenty-five to sit in twos and threes on low, uncomfortable planks. Our boat was painted with two snaky blue-rimmed eyes that stared forward from the prow. A man sat between them, and called back directions to the pilot as we cruised slowly away from the other boats moored at the dock and some children who were swimming after us. Now I think of my own children swimming near an outboard and shiver, but then I was only nervous—and pleasantly nervous—about the young soldier who squatted near the pilot with a submachine gun laid across his lap. This was opium country, northern Thailand, the Golden Triangle. I was there with Peter and Brenda, who worked for a United Nations project that was supposed to convince hill tribe villagers to grow lentils instead of opium poppies. Even Brenda thought the idea was problematic, and she was one of its chief administrators. Peter was more circumspect; he was in public relations. At the moment, that meant shepherding Jack on a press tour of the north: Jack who sat so close to me I knew he had just showered. I wanted to touch him, but of course I could not, and looked back at the dwindling children, the retreating dock, the empty bridge instead.

It was a scintillating morning. The sun was so bright and the sky so painted a blue it felt like we were held inside a crystal. A breathless morning, although there was a cool early breeze that ruffled the hairs of my arms and made me think I was being sprayed with water. Then the boat sped up as we cleared the village and spray did rise, although it proved dank and warm and muddy. Both Jack and I sprang back from it, rubbing shoulders. He smiled at me; I looked down. Jack was a dark, tense man; generically Mediterranean. In this heat he kept his shirt open at the collar to show wiry black hair growing out of skin so transparent that each hair seemed to enter it as a bruise. Jack was a photojournalist; so he said. An American, although his frequent rueful exaggerations might have made you guess Australian.

"Are you ready for this?" he asked, and gestured down the river. I nodded yes, then shook my head no, after we both flushed slightly and I looked down again.

In Toronto I had lived in a communal house that always looked toward the East. In our kitchen alone we had a wok, a cloth picture of Mao kept pinned with the latest button, green tea, rice noodles and anti-Vietnam posters we already treated as artifacts, although the war had only been over for two years. One of the women in our house had been a Buddhist nun in Japan. Mary was vague, competent and cheerful, and she had extraordinary skin that was pallid and freckled yet somehow illuminated, like an old and burnished painting. One night, as she meditated in a Kyoto graveyard, she had met a man playing the shakuhachi over his father's grave. Soon she became pregnant, and when the child was a girl she came home because she did not like the way girls were treated in Japan. It was this same child who later had mud thrown at her on an Edmonton playground, while kids chanted, "Half Jap, half Jap." I suppose Mary felt she could do more to change things in her own country. We all thought we could change things then. We were such hopeful kids: born in the suburbs, educated at university, energetic, important and naïve. Only details escaped us. When two women from the house interviewed Mary about the vacant room, they did not notice the child in the sling underneath her duffel coat. The next night we were surprised to hear a baby cry, but we decided that living with a newborn would be broadening. Broadening: dope was broadening. Macrame was, discussion was. Washing the kitchen floor, no. But travel to the East was the most broadening of all.

So I was in a mood to see the river as luminous that day, bright as eyes, mysterious and fraught. It didn't matter that the water stank, or that we passed a dead dog floating near the shore. I saw emblems, even in the ancient hill tribe women who sat across from us and bailed out the boat. Her skin was so dark and runnelled it made me think about a mountainside eroded by the rain. Then I heard Jack's shutter click.

"Show me those teeth Mama." I turned to find him shooting pictures of the woman.

"Don't," I cried. "Don't make fun of her."

"She's not worried. Look at her, she's completely stoned."

And in fact the woman bailed out the boat with a sleepy, mechanical motion. She spit sometimes. Jack spit too; he could not seem to leave her alone. He shot a whole roll of film of the woman, then fished in his bag for more. But first he found an empty canister, and that seemed to make him think of something. He snapped off its top. Then he began to bail too.

"Don't," I said again. But he did not notice me, and gradually I forgot I was embarrassed when I saw he was not so much making fun of the woman as trying to understand what she was doing. He was after her dissociated piston-like rotation, her mechanical calm. Then he had it, and grinned over at me before he let a mask drop over his face that was an eerie and complete reproduction of the woman's expression. Brenda thought he was cheap and fake; they picked at each other continually. But I took my camera and photographed Jack, then forgot myself enough to photograph the woman too. She looked straight at me with eyes that were tinged brown at the corners. Again I blushed and looked away.

The scenery was different on each side of the river. On Jack's side an open golden savannah undulated south of the riverbank. On mine there were mountains that seemed more arty than real: Chinese scroll mountains, so sudden, parabolas, all looking as if their sides had been quarried away. Now they make me think of the way people all get narrower than we meant to be. Then I thought only about the time I heard Yamumoto-san play his shakuhachi. Yamumoto was the father of my friend Mary's baby. After a year of paperwork he had joined her in Toronto, and we met a weirdly formal man. He usually wore a black suit with short thin pant legs and an even thinner tie. Now he would just need some sunglasses to look like the latest Japanese designer, but those were embellished, rococo times and we did not understand him; he reminded us of the Texas businessmen who had burned Beatles albums. His music seemed even more remote, and it was only when I was boating down the river that I began to understand his playing. Then the mountains made me suddenly feel the beauty of its heart-stopping irrhythm, its plangency that was like the interrupted cries of birds.

The river grew broader and shallower, and at one point, perhaps around noon, it got too shallow to navigate. We had to get out then and walk in water up to our ankles as the crew floated the boat further downstream. The riverbed here was studded with small stones that seemed as vivid as agates under the sparkling water. I stood for a moment to look at them glistening underneath my toes. I preferred to stand, I have sensitive feet, and it was agony for me to walk even the few yards to the place the boatman waited. The pebbles seemed sharp, cruel, tricky, and I had to hold out my arms to keep my balance. Then I felt Jack touch my fingers.

"Shall I take my lady down the dance?" he asked, in a perfect English accent.

We were halfway then to Ban Mai.

Brenda, Peter and I had flown north from Bangkok to Chiang Mai about a week before this. Brenda wanted to go out in the field on a buying trip to some of her model villages. She had local people to do this, but she often set herself ground-level chores, like a company president putting his son into the stockroom, or a Chinese bureaucrat sent into the countryside during the Cultural Revolution. Brenda was just as apt to explain herself one way as the other. When she came home she started an import company that paid high prices to Thai artisans while still turning a nice profit; enough, at any rate, to pay for Peter's humour magazine. Brenda and Peter had lived in my Toronto house several turnovers before. I knew them from the times they stayed with us on homeleaves, and when I quit my first job and bought an around-the-world ticket they invited me to Bangkok, even though they must have known my curiosity would be nearly as exhausting as my opinions.

I can still see Brenda leaning against the doorframe of her Chiang Mai office. She was tall and lanky and freckled, and her expression was characteristically that of a schoolgirl. Disgust was barely withheld, bewilderment politely exaggerated. The district manager had just asked her to take Jack along on her trip.

"I'm really pretty harmless," Jack said, and smiled at her charmingly. He should have known better: Peter was there, and it should have been obvious she liked a different kind of man. But Jack looked surprised when she turned away and began speaking to a secretary. He made a wry face at her back, which he exaggerated when he realized I saw it.

"I suppose we need all sorts of publicity," Brenda agreed finally, when she turned back. I enjoyed her rudeness when it was directed at people in charge, but this did not seem fair. Jack looked so vulnerable with his letter of accreditation hanging in one hand and his feet, in blue and yellow running shoes, planted slightly apart on the cool stone floor. I frowned at Brenda. She shook her shoulders dismissively.

Brenda and I had not been getting along. In fact the last time we had spent an hour without bickering was on the drive into Bangkok from the airport the night we first arrived. I was giddy then, still unused to the fruity, moist, diesel smell of Oriental cities. I laughed at each garishly painted truck, each weedy, slick canal. Then we turned into their driveway and I saw the car lights flash on the high white walls of a compound. On UN salaries Peter and Brenda had a cook, a gardener, a laundress and a maid, all of whom waited on us with averted eyes and the subtly withheld air of servitude. I did not like it. Or rather, I could not approve of the way they lived, not least because it made me feel like I was visiting my parents. Comfort, guilt and condescension were a mixture I thought I had rejected for a purer and poorer life, and I thought Peter and Brenda had rejected too. When they first came to Bangkok as student volunteers they kept a small apartment and no maid. But Brenda said when they got their more powerful UN jobs they were asked to get a house where they could entertain.

"The servants came with the house," she said. "What would you have us do? Fire them?"

It was the same tone she used with Jack the next morning, when we were getting ready to leave. He came around the corner of the UN building just as the workers scrambled into the big green truck that was to follow us up into the hills. He was not late enough to have kept us waiting, or early enough to have got in the way, or even so punctiliously on time that he offended against local inexactitude, but Brenda still seemed annoyed to see him. She started our jeep with a roar as soon as he had said hello and climbed into the seat behind her.

"So, how far to the first village?" he asked, leaning over her shoulder.

"That depends on what happened to the road during the last rains."

"What usually happens?"

"Lots."

I had braided my hair after my shower. I thought that Jack might notice, but Brenda teased him until he was half draped over her seat, questioning her persistently, playfully, angrily, slyly and ignoring everything else. I grew pettish. Maybe they were feeling a subterranean attraction that left me out. But when Peter laughed quietly it occurred to me that this was just the sort of jostling for superiority that can go on without sex; at least it passed that way in a pair of men.

Soon we felt the plain around Chiang Mai and began to climb into the nearby mountains. The road became a raw, red, bulldozed track; the trees an intense and glassy green.

"How would you describe the villages?"

"National Geographic land."

And in fact we found airy bamboo houses on stilts. Pigs lay under them, while goats with yellow eyes strolled by and children tumbled out their doors like sparrows. We spent a week going into villages like this one, all of them built on mountain clearings: some recent, some more overgrown. I thought each looked from a distance like a child's spilled toys. The houses were miniature, their placement haphazard. I said I was charmed. Brenda told me the mortality statistics.

That first day the headman greeted us from the doorway of the largest house in the village. Farmers squatted around him; women stood further back. The formalities started even as we waded through the children, but they were brief, this was business, and before too long Brenda and the headman began to dicker loudly about the price she would pay for the crop. Brenda spoke in English and used a translator, but I could not understand the rhythm of these negotiations. Farmers stood up and left in what I thought were the middle of sentences. Others repeatedly showed her the same dusty-looking bowl of lentils. Squatting, spitting, restless, they all watched Brenda intently. Her auburn hair was just the colour of the women's faded scarves. Then they finally reached a deal, and she peeled bills to pay them from a gambler's roll of *baht.*

This went on for close to a week. Brenda dickered, and while she did so Jack dolleyed around her with his camera. He was smooth and insistent and sometimes intrusive as he lay on the ground to shoot up for a picture. Peter laughed at him.

"Is this the new trend where a journalist inserts himself into the story?"

I had to agree he overdid it, but as the days passed I stopped minding, because I began to believe he did it for me.

We sat together in the back of the jeep each morning on

those long and bumpy rides into the mountains. At first Jack was only friendly. Yet there was something suggestive in the very fact of sitting together for so long that began to make itself felt. We grew conscious of each other, then self-conscious, awkward, shy and apologetic. When bad jolts on the rutted road made Jack's camera bag fly against me, he was too quick to grab it back. One time we both blushed in surprise to see a dusty white scratch a buckle left on my knee. I grew hopeful, particularly when he began to expect me to help him with his work. I held the different lenses, and finally left Brenda and Peter behind to hike with him up into the poppy fields.

These poppy fields grew side by side with fields of Brenda's lentils on the outskirts of every village. No-one blamed the farmers; they were poor and had to hedge their bets. Besides, the fields were lovely, as dreamy and drowsy as the one where Dorothy slept on her way to Oz. Normally the farmers hiked up there in the morning, and cut the ripe hips of the poppies using peculiar knives with three sharp blades. They waited all day for the opium sap to ooze out, then went back up in the evening to collect it in leather pouches, which they would later sell to buyers in the heroin trade. Jack wanted to telescope this process. Each time he grew tired of Brenda's dickering he would collect a farmer in traditional dress and take him up into the fields. While I held the camera, he posed him with his pouch or knife. I knew I wasn't much help, but this was almost the point. Since he didn't need me, he must want me. Whenever he looked my way I smiled.

Soon Jack began to turn to me with shy little facts an older woman would have recognized as boasting.

"This reminds me of Vietnam," he said once, as we drove through the lowlands.

"It's odd," Brenda called back. "With the number of veterans you meet over here, you'd think they would have won the bloody war."

"Steady on," Peter told her.

"I was there all right," Jack murmured, and I risked patting his shoulder. He smiled back slightly, and when I found I had to look away again I saw Brenda observing us both shrewdly in the rear-view mirror. Then she smiled too, kindly and sadly and protectively. I don't know what I brought back to her, but it is true she has remained very tenaciously married herself.

Our last day-trip from Chiang Mai was arranged to show Jack one of the Thai king's agricultural projects. Peter had angled for a Prince to meet us there, a cousin or second cousin of the King, and all the way through the mountains, Jack worried about what we should call him.

"Maybe I'll just call him Prince."

"Here Prince," Peter called. "Sit Prince. Shake a paw."

"I refuse to call anyone Your Highness."

"Kneel Prince before the American empire. Propaganda division. Ministry," Peter said precisely, "of disinformation." Brenda interrupted.

"In private conversation, Queen Elizabeth is called ma'am." She seemed to be making a joke, although I could not see what it was, or understand at first why Jack laughed so maliciously. But then he started one of his mimes. He began to sip tea with his finger crooked in what sometimes seemed a parody of the Queen and sometimes a dig at Brenda. It was a weird, flickering performance. Sometimes the two came together in a mean dual portrait, but sometimes he was just bad. Brenda still seemed angry though, even when he'd stopped.

"Sometimes I'll get it right," Jack told me complacently.

We reached the project in mid-afternoon. It was in a high and distant valley. Green mountains rose around us, and I do not know how this can be, but the farthest ones seemed just as green. The air was as clear as cold but it was not cold.

I thought it was an astonishing place. Plum trees seemed to drift up the mountains, they stirred so, and shimmered in a light breeze. Slow and drugged-looking insects bumbled everywhere, and the cinnamon smell from acres of carnations burned in our noses like fire. We got out of the jeep almost breathlessly, and were soon joined by the Prince, who came out of the station bungalow. Now I saw Brenda's joke. The Prince was a slender, effeminate man, who was tall for a Thai and very elegant in a tailored silk safari suit. Five Buddhist threads of rank were tied around one wrist. The other he used wearily to stroke his face, which was decadent and shrewd and tired. This was just another press tour. Already he was bored.

Peter and I were quickly the opposite. Normally Peter was a benign and courteous man, but that day both he and I seemed to grow drunk on the heavy air.

"Here Prince," he called. "Can you tell me the name of this flower here?"

The Prince ignored him. Instead he concentrated on Jack, who in a weird reversal seemed as mild as Peter usually appeared, and just as eager to listen. In time he even seemed impressed, then wilted, abject in the presence of what so many Americans seem to think is the real thing, the genuine article, a hereditary aristocracy; which of course isn't real at all, but only a symbol. I was disappointed in Jack. I wanted him to be more cynical. But I didn't do anything until the Prince put his hand on Jack's neck to guide him around a bed of pink lilies. Jack looked sheepish but he took nothing back, and suddenly I was sick of the station, of its sweetness and unreality, and went back alone to the car. Soon Peter joined me and leaned against the door. He was more subdued now too.

"When they fire me," he began ruefully, "I suppose we'll just have to learn to live on Brenda's salary. Retrench. Fire the servants. Eat chicken feet and rice."

The others soon returned.

"Can you use one of these?" Brenda was asking Jack, as she handed him her camera. She wanted a picture of herself with the Prince in the field of flowers. Jack clowned a little as he took three or four shots.

"Please," the Prince said then, and reached for the camera. He shooed the rest of us over to Brenda. "You look so very North American," he said from behind the camera. "I should really use a wide-angle lens to encompass your broad horizons." After that we left.

Brenda got the film developed after we flew back to Bangkok.. The pictures the Prince had taken were perfectly in focus, while the ones by Jack were no good at all.

"I knew he was a fake," Brenda crowed. "I knew it. I said so."

"He used a Pentax himself, not a Nikon," Peter said. "Although I suppose a real pro would know how to use whatever you threw at him." I said nothing myself. Once I would have defended him, however weakly, but this was after we had been to Ban Mai.

The river landing was inconspicuous and the village itself not visible from the water. All we could see was the small, rocky, honey-coloured crescent of sand our boat finally nosed onto. I can still hear and feel the sand grit like cinders under the prow of that boat. It reminded me of every time I landed a canoe: a festive sound, a promising tension. We clambered out and stretched our legs, while behind us the villagers flicked into the forest and disappeared.

I now keep a photograph of Ban Mai on my kitchen wall to look at when my children are too rowdy or my life seems intolerably mundane: two conditions that intersect, gavotte, spark off each other in a prism of refracted irritability that sometimes seems to have become the deepest thing about me. Yet that picture proves I was somewhere else once; something more, so it seemed. It shows three boy monks. They are really only students, not postulates, although they wear the religious robe in three shades of much-washed saffron. The one in the middle has jug ears; all three wear rubber thongs and stand on a brown bit of hillside that is dusted with ashes from the previous night's bonfire. I stood near the sight of that bonfire to take my picture. Behind me was a hilltop temple made of cinderblocks with two enormous speakers on its top. Inside that temple on the first day was a jumble of women squatting and chatting on the floor. Some were stringing marigolds, some were cradling children. It struck me as faintly irreligious then, but now I recognize the pugnacious familiarity of a ladies' auxiliary at work. These women came from the bamboo and palm-leaf houses scattered down the hill on which my boy monks stood. But the houses are not visible in the photograph. There is just a ravine of banana trees and papery purple bougainvillea, its flowers looking crisp and dyed; of creepers, mangoes, vines and saplings that reach the boys' thin waists. Behind them, behind the ravine on a more distant hillside, is a plantation of those hopeful white flowering plums. If you look closely, you can see tools lying around them on the ground. Above it all, capping my photograph, dominating the scene are the vague, lumpen mountains that wash blue, grey, blurry into the misty sky.

The mountains are in Burma. Ban Mai is a village of refugees, of Shan people who are fighting the Burmese army in an ambiguous war over territory just north of the border, or some say control of the heroin trade. We went there for the Shan New Year's Day celebrations, just as tourists, packing our cameras and bedrolls into the village guesthouse. And it was partly this holiday atmosphere that began to prod Jack and me into something more, partly the fact that Peter insisted on coming along on our rambles through the brief streets of the village. He had so completely the air of a chaperone that we began to flirt to tease him. There is nothing better than a shared joke to feed a flirtation and Peter was that: benign, dogged, a bit worried, and probably insincere; mocking and satirical in a way that turned the joke on us for being so young. Peter's role in this whole trip was quite unclear. He had never taken seriously the impressive letter of accreditation Jack had presented in Chiang Mai, and it is possible he used his initial position as escort really to keep an eye on Jack, as a combustible commodity, in the same way he did now in Ban Mai by playing so hennishly the role of chaperone. The village was really quite tiny. It did not take long to explore, and soon we settled down on the guesthouse stairs to watch the villagers go by in their cut-offs and sarongs. The children ran past us on long, bare, skinny legs; the adults all walked slowly, and if I turned my head to just the right angle I could watch both them and Jack, who sat below me on the steps and sometimes wiped the tender bruised and sweaty skin in the hollow of his throat. We seemed to have all the time in the world. Sometimes it felt as if we travelled to get thankfully, pleasantly tired, then sit in the shade with a beer.

Occasionally Brenda walked past us. She was a wonderful photographer, whose pictures seemed so casual and unposed that when you looked at them you got an idea of what the people in them had actually experienced, rather than feeling what she felt when she watched. In Ban Mai there was an outdoor shower surrounded by screens of woven palm leaves. In the afternoon a monk went in, and soon he hung his robe over the screen while shuffling his bare brown feet underneath it. I leapt up from the steps while Jack murmured encouragement to take a picture of the screen, the robe, the feet, as if there were something unusual in a man taking a shower. Brenda's picture on the other hand made the scene look ordinary. A dirt road meanders past the shower. To the front is a woman who thinks she is not in the picture and looks down distractedly. A dog sits nearby, licking his parts. To the rear a bare-chested boy stares belligerently into the camera with two stiff arms partly raised at his sides. This is such a distance from my three posed, uneasy boys. I came East thinking I would not act like a typical tourist. I would observe and not impose, but my picture is taken; I *took,* while Brenda just seemed to pick things up and put them back again. Maybe that is why she was accepted in the hill tribe villages, although the position of women there is traditionally low. She had what was seen as a masculine disinterestedness; women were thought to be more grasping. That first night in Ban Mai the headman even proclaimed her an honorary man, although he hesitated before he did the same with me, perhaps because he saw a vulnerability that I have been slow to recognize in myself.

When I recall Thailand it comes usually as a silent memory of lyrical lines and ceaselessly flowing figures, but that first night was rough and rude, and to think of it brings back undiminished the sounds—the hawking spits into the corner of the headman's house—the smell of kerosene lanterns, their hiss, the smart of impure smoke, the strangeness of the village men in the circle of white light: their faces reduced to planes and shadows, their fingers to oddly arching bones. We had been asked there to have a drink with the headman. The liquor was as raw and oily as his son, who had been to Chiang Mai and acquired an unholy jumble of languages that let him more or less translate his father's insinuating toasts. I say insinuating because the headman recognized Brenda as an employee of the UN and was intent on appropriating her as an official representative to the Shan celebration, which she was not and did not want to be. Her own toasts were sinuous speeches of polite disclaimer, which were such masterpieces of diplomatic unspeak that once Jack clapped lightly, almost soundlessly, in appreciation.

Jack sat very close beside me on the floor. We were

packed in, and sometimes as he uncrossed and recrossed his legs uncomfortably he nudged me, so that even though we were in the darkest corner of the room he seemed as angular and pointed as the most starkly lit men. I could not forget him, particularly when it got very late and I felt sick and drunk and pleasant, and he reached to take my hand. He took it unobtrusively, not as comfort or connection but exploration. I felt electrified. I could not even look at Jack, although it seemed as if I could feel every whorl of his fingers. Then, when I finally struggled up the nerve and smiled at him, I was both relieved and disappointed to find that for the moment he was looking away.

I remembered then the guesthouse had one room. We were to sleep, all four of us, on the floor. Every other night on our travels we had returned to the best hotel in Chiang Mai. I had hated it. It was too posh, too bourgeois for my idea of myself. When we were shown the guesthouse in Ban Mai I thought it was much more suitable. Yet it seemed the opposite now, even when Jack took back his hand and moved away without ever having looked at me. I remained alive to him, especially when the toasts finally ended and we stumbled back through the dark village to the guesthouse. I wondered what would happen. Yet when we got inside Jack lay down and fell almost immediately into a deep and healthy sleep. I felt chagrined. It was insulting, and somehow inappropriate, suggestive, disturbing to find so soon he slept in a childlike curl with one arm thrown out, and one hand fallen vulnerably open. I could not sleep for wanting to touch him, and for the whine of the tropical animals outside, for the utter strangeness of lying in a hut a few miles south of Burma, among people whose habits seemed random and unpredictable to me. I felt afraid—not least that I *would* touch him—and my eventual sleep was full of odd, questing dreams. I woke up the next morning feeling nervous and disoriented, even before I realized that Jack had withdrawn to his previous light flirtatiousness, which seemed as much a response to Peter as to me.

This was the day of the Shan celebrations, although we did not know what these would consist of, nor when they would start. This made the villagers' most everyday occupations—eating rice and pumpkin, drawing water, bathing in bowls on their stairs—seem heavy and obscure, as if they were taking part in an opera, or playing a strange extended sport with complicated rules. Children set off firecrackers in the dirt streets. The headman's son, who had attached himself to us as a sort of cultural ambassador, nodded at them significantly, and made even this simple and familiar celebration seem weighted. The time went slowly, and the unfulfilled expectation I felt toward Jack became general; the day seemed splintered, breathtaking and odd. Strange times, made stranger in the late afternoon by a sudden mechanical clatter overhead and the descent of a helicopter into a field that only then took on the dimensions of an airstrip. The Prince we had met before emerged, and was greeted by a delegation of officials. With him was a young Eurasian man he soon introduced as his nephew. No-one was fooled. The young man was very beautiful, and walked something like a sailor. He was my age; Jack's age.

It did not take me long to wonder whether Jack was really homosexual. He and the nephew took to each other from the start, and began to pal around the village. I was not sure; it could also have been that the nephew brought some marijuana and Jack, it turned out, liked to smoke. They disappeared frequently into the forest and came out high and funky. Sometimes the headman's son trailed after them; occasionally I made an abject fourth. But even this did not make Jack notice me. His flirtatiousness had evaporated, and I felt like last week's toy. Yet I could keep away from them no more than could the Prince, with whom I felt a sudden odd identity. I had travelled halfway around the world that year, but for all my romanticism about the workers, and my equally romantic, Roundhead rejection of the aristocracy, I never stepped outside the middle class until that day in Ban Mai, when I stood watching the nephew and Jack jostle companionably across town. Then I caught the eye of the Prince, and left class behind when I saw in his face a sick jealousy that was the same as my own.

As it turned out, the Shan celebrations started at sundown. Around that time people began to drift up the hill toward the temple in a casual and friendly stream. Soon we joined them, and near the top Brenda put our blanket on the ground. A bonfire began to blaze behind us; officials emerged from the temple and started to speak. But it was not an organized production. The officials spoke from no platform and to no particular audience; like us, the villagers were just settling in, and they chatted and rustled in small groups. The headman's son and a ragtag crew tried to start a portable generator, but before they could do so, the speeches were finished, the officials sat down, and on another part of the hillside some women rose and began to dance. Theirs was the symbolic underwater dance where each slow movement of the fingers and neck was in itself a ritual. They were hypnotic; I thought of shorebirds moving incrementally through a lagoon, lifting each leg so smoothly it did not ripple the surface of the water. Then there was a crackle from the loudspeakers as the generator clicked on, and we were suddenly listening to the Doobie Brothers. The night was like that. A thick sky black as treacle was broken by fireworks, which flared and faded in one brief grand display. A movie screen was put up. First there was a propaganda short warning against the use of marijuana, during which the Prince stood beside the screen with his arms crossed. After that they showed *From Here to Eternity* with the reels out of order, while an amateur magician performed nearby and we listened to periodic songs from a choir of sleepy children. I was enthralled; outside myself for once. I hardly noticed that the hillside was cold and the bonfire smoky. Nor did I feel much when Jack finally appeared and insinuated himself beside me on the ground.

I suppose I had finally recognized him as one of those men who are ashamed of what they want, although I was not yet old enough to realize that this was his problem and not mine. Certainly I felt sore about the way he had treated me, but most of my attention was elsewhere and I found I had no more need of him. Literally that: I had no need, I was already being satisfied, and it had anyway occurred to me to wonder where one went when Peter and Brenda were in the same room , and the bush was full of snakes. When he began to nudge me again, I edged away. It is silly to think of. He nudged, I shuffled off, and when he saw what I was doing he mimicked my shuffle with a cruel twist that made me look timid and shrinking. Then he laughed and took my hand. I snatched it back and he laughed again, before leaning on me heavily. He smiled like a burning garden.

"You know what you are?" he confided. "You're just a tease."

I got up angrily and flounced over to Peter and Brenda. Brenda put one hand kindly on my shoulder, although it seemed to me that in the shadows, Peter quietly laughed. We did not stay long after this, and soon got up stiffly to make our way through the undiminished crowd. But it annoyed me to see that Jack stood up too, and left the nephew sitting by the Prince in the flickering blue light cast by the movie screen. He joined us as we stumbled through the moonlit village, and I thought he walked too close behind me as we went up the guesthouse stairs. Still, I did not see what he could do with Peter and Brenda there beside me, and in fact he seemed to drop off quickly, despite the sound of Peter's snoring. I could not sleep myself. The snoring, the thudding entertainment on the hill, the pigs, the crowing roosters, the monkeys in the jungle: all kept me awake. Then Jack made a sound too as he lay so close beside me on the floor. Or perhaps it was not so much a sound as a change in his breathing, a restlessness that was not quite restless sleeping, a disturbance that seemed almost a moan. I thought he was masturbating. I could think nothing else, and soon I grew so disgusted with him and myself that I was close to crying with anger. He grew louder. He was not so loud really, under Peter's snores, but I heard each breath and each one seemed insistent to me. Then maybe he heard some change in my breathing too, or maybe I was wrong and he really was asleep, but the insistence grew unmistakable; it grew beseeching and abandoned and theatric, until suddenly the moaning formed into words.

"No please. No, no please. Please don't. *Please* don't. Please please please." Then he sat up abruptly and sank back down again.

The next morning, Jack was nervous, smug and apologetic.

"I guess I had one of my nightmares last night." He confided to me proudly, " Vietnam."

When we got back to Chiang Mai, I was happy to check into the best hotel in town. I was too emotionally exhausted to remember what was wrong with lying on lounges that were just like the lounges I lay on at home. I did not want any more Thai food either. I wanted hamburgers, french fries, milkshakes: the Thais make lovely ice cream. It was only a small change, a tiny step, but it seems to me sometimes that these small steps can never be retaken, and it is the big ones that are much more easily retraced. Yamumoto-san the shakuhachi player went back to Japan after an unsuccessful year in Canada. He married a woman his family chose for him and has since become a successful musician. My friend Mary told me their daughter Mika once wrote him a letter, but he has never answered. Mika is a lovely girl. It is also probably true that the big steps are the best ones.

Our final day in Chiang Mai was clear and warm and golden. I spent it by the pool. In fact I was lying there drinking a Coke when Jack came out to say goodbye. Seeing him unexpectedly like that made me remember he was just my type. He carried a small parcel tied with string, and opened it when all his other sallies failed.

"I wanted to show you," he said. It was a length of Thai silk, which was blue and green at the same time, and heavy as long hair. It rippled like hair too, and seemed to flow and shimmer. "You have such good taste," Jack said shyly. "What do you think? It's for my girlfriend in San Francisco."

Peter and Brenda came out just after that. Peter smiled and dropped into a chair while signalling for a beer. Brenda sat down protectively beside me. Jack talked for a while about Hong Kong, where he said he was heading. Then he left, and left the Thai silk lying casually in its package. Peter tried to call him back, but Jack only waved and kept going as if he had heard nothing, although I was certain that he had. I also knew there was no girlfriend in San Francisco. I recognized the parcel as his attempt at an excuse, although it was only later, when I was kinder, that I learned to call it an apology.

Miracles

When I was in the fourth grade, back in the suburbs, we kept lined, half-sized exercise books called our vocabulary books. Our teacher said to surprise her with new words, although I doubt we ever did. Miss Jackson had already taught elementary school for six or seven years. She was a little longer getting married than most, a little more angular, and we children had not changed much in her time. We were pretty exclusively white, middle class, Anglo Saxon, largely and mildly Protestant; the predictable children of comfortable parents, as rosy and commonplace as robins. Even our vocabulary books were mild: the cheekiest boys only wrote in "fart." Jamie Murray did that, and went to great trouble with the library dictionary over his definition. "Intestinal," Miss Jackson only drawled. "Very impressive, Jamie." She had a bouffant hairdo and thick, wicked, slashing eyeliner, like an Egyptian tomb painting or the Gabor sisters. She wore dungarees outside of school, and one year impressed us right into the ground when she took a tour of Europe. Took a tour; I think now the boredom of teaching elementary school must be somewhat lightened by seeing your small adventures daily seem marvellous.

Some of the girls had crushes on Miss Jackson. We all had crushes then, and uniforms. That is, navy tunics with the yokes still flat, screechingly starched white blouses with Peter Pan collars, navy knee socks and—not required, but *comme il faut*—black-and-white saddle shoes, painstakingly polished, the white polish watery and smelling of chalk, tasting, when we licked our fingers, something like peppermint. Scorn was also big. *Scorn out,* we cried. At Micky Hanson, who also wrote "fart," then tore a hole right through the paper when he tried to rub it out. And Fiona Mackie. Fiona had a crush on Miss Jackson that was just be*yond.* Maybe so. I saw Fiona a few years ago on a television program about mental illness. She followed a particular actress around. The psychiatrist they interviewed afterward seemed startled by her firmness, but we had known about Fiona. I especially feared her, seeing something in myself. It was not my feeling for Miss Jackson, which was suitably there, but also suitably restrained; more a susceptibility, I think, rooted in our vocabulary books. But I loved words, and to love something inanimate was too solitary and hopeless, like going to live in a tree.

Words. I loved a series of them; I was serially monogamous. Antidisestablishmentarianism. Then prejudice: a succession of syllables I did not understand. But there was also a more precious word, a secret word. Miracles. I do not mean to cast doubt on at least the intentions of the United Church of Canada. I must have heard that word before from my Sunday-school teacher Mrs. Hargreaves. But Mrs. Hargreaves had buck teeth and worked as a clerk at the five-and-ten. She was meek and stooped; there were rumours that her husband beat her, although this might only have been the certainty that he could have, and she would not have complained. Perhaps I learned about brutality from Mrs. Hargreaves, but I did not learn about miracles. That happened one day in regular school, when Miss Jackson stood in front of the class, all cheekbones, nerves and eyeliner.

"Children, Micky Hanson's mother has—died, passed away."

It was all over school by recess that she had jumped from the Second Narrows Bridge. The school secretary spoke of the nineteen men who had been killed during its construction, and said it was a sin for this living woman to choose to die when any one of the nineteen would happily have traded places with her. How this could have been arranged, she did not say, but her thought made the day seem stranger. We were all displaced, seasick. It was as if an earthquake had fractured the school, then put it back together clumsily, so the walls did not quite meet. That dizzying, open crack took our breath; it sucked it out as a long, sickening, drawn-out, "How?"

"Her head squashed bam when she hit the water," Fiona Mackie said in a hugely satisfied, proprietory voice.

"Silly. It was water. It was soft. It was like diving from the rocks in Hawaii," I insisted. "She *drownded.*" I wanted a perfect body, unbruised, merely sleeping.

It would have been easier if it was someone regular's mother, so there could have been an antiseptic feel to the death. We could have folded our hands piously and seen sunbeams, fleecy clouds, a pastel, Sunday-school Heaven where barefoot, blue-robed Jesus walked upon rocks that were astonishing in their warm look of smoothness, their bland forgiving greyness. We could have forgotten about it then. But it was Micky Hanson's mother, so there was something earthy about it. At lunchtime the boys talked too loudly about worms. There were fights on the playground that ended with exaggerated sobbing. And I sat on a cement wall, where I opened my lunchbucket with its permanent, oily smell of bananas. My mother had packed a thermos of soup, a sandwich, a MacIntosh apple, a piece of chocolate cake.

Given the extraordinary nature of the day, I opened the cake first. It was in waxed paper that crinkled into the icing and tore it off, so normally you could eat the icing separately. Now I just looked at it. Ten is perhaps a bit young for me to have understood that I, personally, will die, but that is how circumstances fell out. I saw earth. I saw it thrown on top of my open mouth, my open eyes; light, crumbling, smothering as peat. Then Miss Jackson walked by with another teacher, speaking stridently. "If that boy turns out now," she said, "it will be a miracle."

The word hit me. It blazed with sudden memories of Moses and his burning bush. It gleamed like loaves and fishes rising from a turquoise sea. I felt the promise, the beauty in the word. And looked up to a crystal spring day. The roof of the school cut clean into the sky, while the sun bounced off its windows so they seemed to call back, agreeing. Below them, the asphalt of the playground was black as black; the legs of all the children pink and plump as candy. I could not imagine what could be more wonderful than earth, more heady than life. It all seemed such a miracle to me.

That afternoon I lived through class on the edge of happy crying. Then at three o'clock I fled with the bell and ran joyously up the hall. I panted and sweat and heard my heart beat in my ears. I ran, loving the pressure of my fat knees pumping. I ran past home, to the end of the block, to the ravine and its creek. I half lived there in the summer, and if it was too lush to know every tree, every hummock, I had my places: my bridge of stones across the shallow-running creek, my hidey holes, my climbing tree; I knew where there were ground wasps worth avoiding. That day I ran quickly through the pass between the houses, down the slope, my feet pad-pad-padding on the loosely packed floor like those of a cantering animal. I had my arms up as I ran so the afternoon air licked through my fingers and tickled the sweat. It defined me, letting me know: these are my hands, my fingers, my own arms. I saw everything so cleanly. When I stopped, near the bottom of the slope, I saw the clear creek coursing over stones, making small rapids that foamed and bubbled like lace, like a lace made of beads, each sparkling, glinting in the sun. The cedar trees around it had bark split into marvellous patterns, like glass that had been shattered, but stood together still. I crouched. On the forest floor under trees there were tiny starflowers blooming. Each had three leaves on a slender green stalk, and rising above this was a miniature stem of flowers, the stem so thin it was like an eyelash painfully extended; the flowers fairy flowers, they were so small, so pink, so translucent. Miracle, I thought. The world is a miracle.

There was a tree nearby we had made into a jungle jim, a maple just as thick as my leg, which we had bent down and tied with ropes, so it arched off the forest floor and down again. I ran to it now and began to walk across it with my hands, low at first, but then hanging and swinging my feet off the ground. I felt the smooth, papery bark chafe my palms. I felt the pull of gravity through my walking arms, my hanging legs, my innocent, dangling feet. And with this I felt my muscles stretch and my blood flow so quickly and forcefully that I felt fully alive. Miracle, I thought. I am a miracle. And I felt this so strongly, so powerfully, that I thought of projecting it onto Micky Hanson's mother. I would make her breathe again. But the thought made me sick. It made me drop to the ground, with a chumpf! when my feet hit. That was wrong. It was extreme. I had a sudden awareness of Fiona Mackie, not as if I had seen her so much as become her. I would not do that. Instead I built a wall in my head against the idea. I looked at the bracken now in front of me, the moss green of its leaves, the soft, yellow rounds of spores that were like the pads on the paws of animals. *There* was the miracle. I would see that far, and no further.

This became my policy for the longest time. I would live in the present and build a great wall at its boundary, at the place of possibilities. Once, when I was home sick from school, I built a wall in the way of my cat having kittens. I was lying in bed. The spread was tucked smooth, the pink papered walls seemed to glow with my fever. The cat was sleeping nearby, on the beige rug. Suddenly she growled, not in warning but surprise; a very salty, female sound. I knew she was going to have her kittens, and looked down to see wetness on the rug, before I turned away. I turned away, I would not watch, refused to see. Only when I heard the sound of licking did I turn back and watch her wash a thistly grey bundle. I don't know what my cat sensed; cats sense things. But when she was finished, she picked up her kitten by the scruff of its neck and carried it out of my bedroom. She had the other two in her box in the basement.

Another time my mother was mowing the lawn in the back yard. It was a big yard, a grassy meadow with foxgloves growing underneath the chestnut trees. We had an old gas mower that sputtered and smelled, and once threw a stone through my bedroom window. On the day I am speaking of, it sputtered out. Mr. Hudspeth from next door was leaning over the fence and saw this. The Hudspeths were an over-blown family with five children, one of whom was fat. All of them fought, Mr. and Mrs. Hudspeth so loudly that sometimes my father had to close all the windows. That day Mr. Hudspeth offered to fix the mower, and leapt the fence like one of his kids. I was playing nearby, punching the necks of foxgloves so their stamens gaped, but he did not seem to see me. He knelt by the mower and talked only to my mother, efficiently at first, then more and more disconnectedly, forgetfully, until I heard him say, "Oh June," and realized he was crying. I turned then and ran away.

When I said earlier that we were all alike in the suburbs, I both believed that and didn't. I have a gallery of exceptions: jaunty Miss Jackson, poor religious Mrs. Hargreaves, the next-door Hudspeths, Micky Hanson, Fiona Mackie, even my cat; of course, especially, myself. Yet I have here one of those black-and-white photographs they took every school year, with all of us lined up in rows. And it is true to this extent: Fiona Mackie has a loopy smile. Her hair is half combed, a droopy cardigan hangs skew-whiff across her tunic. But I see that Miss Jackson looks merely young for her age, and not so much nervous as anxious. I am unkind. I see her finally getting married, breathing out, letting go at the waist, relaxing. Micky Hanson I have trouble finding at first. But then I think I see him in a rather ordinary-looking boy, who is only slightly, ridiculously plump around the hips. I do not remember that, but now I think it is the simple cause of all our taunting. I could do this with all of them: mild, serviceable Mrs. Hargreaves, the Hudspeths, who had spats. And myself? In the photograph, I sit in the girls' front row on a gym bench. My feet are demurely crossed, I have my hands in my lap the way we've been told. Like the other girls, I seem primarily ingratiating. If you look more closely, you can see one knee sock has fallen slightly lower than the other, a sign, perhaps, of carelessness. I can claim no more distinction than that.

2

I left my husband. I think I might be the first person to leave a husband because he was too intelligent, understanding, charming, ambitious—or rather because he was all these things, and I was bored. This is a joke I tell on myself. My failed marriage.

It gets closer to the truth to say I left Kim because I found I could not have children. We were living in Montreal at the time. Briefly, in an ugly furnished apartment without proper curtains. I was not working, but to get out of the apartment, I developed an interest in churches. I could always be counted on to develop an interest in something. We had been married for eight years, and moving for most of them, so I had got into the habit of curiosity. It wasn't too bad. In fact I said I liked Kim's transfers, because they gave me a chance to sample cities and jobs, to find out what I really wanted in life. I see my past self as cheerful, never complaining; a small, dark-haired robin of a woman, confident this was what one did in life: one learned. In Montreal, I learned about churches. Surely it is not too odd to develop an interest in churches when you are having the trouble I was having getting pregnant.

It started one overcast day in August, shortly after we arrived. A grey day, heavy as mercury, when I went out for a walk near St. Urbain Street. I had read about the old Jewish quarter then in Mordecai Richler's novels, and was drawn to its pungency and tenuousness, which were so foreign to my suburban life. As I walked slowly by, I tested a sort of rueful feeling that if you had grown up here, you would be left with problems it might take a lifetime to solve, which would anyway grant you some purpose. It was partly Portuguese now, still poor, still with the flying metal stairways and the shanty-like additions out the back. I saw few people. But as I rambled through an alley, I caught the sound of singing through an open back doorway. A single sound: a cantor in a synagogue, so rich and yearning in his song that I closed my eyes and breathed lightly to hear him. I closed my eyes, yet I had the sensation of still seeing, of looking up to a movie-blue sky with fat white clouds rushing on it. As the cantor's voice grew higher and higher, then slid and soared, my eyes seemed to trace those rushing clouds along their swift edges. I felt my eyes roll under my closed lids. I felt myself roll up there with the clouds and wind, all free and cool and tumbling until there were no eyes, no ears, no song, just the glide of sailing up so high, the teasing, daunting, daring ride of a cry toward heaven.

There is something in other peoples' churches it seems no longer possible to find in one's own. The unexplained, I suppose, although given my experience, this is probably for the best. I did not even try to find a United Church in Montreal. I could not believe in blond wood pews. Instead, searching for the ease I found that afternoon, I began to go to Catholic churches. Once, to a storefront tabernacle where they talked in tongues; spooky as player pianos. It was disingenuous of me to say earlier that I developed an interest in churches. In fact I began to need them. I needed their discipline, to stop me from experimenting with the idea there was something wrong with my marriage. Kim was a successful man and a busy one. But lately the broad plane of his cheekbones had made him look to me like one of those tall glass buildings: the kind birds fly into. When I sat across from him in the evening, my eyes seemed to slide down his blond hair and smooth shoulders, down his knit green polo shirts, his worn jeans, his runners, but they would no longer lie on the ground at his feet. In the churches, I tried for acceptance, but often I just found more time to think. I saw that if this kept on, I could become like my old Sunday-school teacher Mrs. Hargreaves: prematurely bent and quaintly pious. I straightened my shoulders militantly. But from that experimental start, I developed something of the same attitude toward Kim that Mrs. Hargreaves must have had toward her husband, whom she let the world think beat her.

Other people who go to Montreal, tourists (as I was more or less), always go to one church: the Oratory on the slopes of Mount Royal. It is sacred to St. Joseph and to Brother André, who in his lifetime was a handyman there and now, it is said, performs miracles. The Oratory lies at the top of three monumental banks of stairs. It is an immense building, which rambles up the hillside in layers that have been added over the years. For me, though, the corporate effect is of the late fifties and early sixties. It is solid, almost smug. I would even call it suburban. The spareness isn't grand because it's so concrete, and it doesn't seem to lift the sky as Gothic churches do. The movement is down, the colours are muddy. And I am afraid of it, because of its resonances. Both the suburban look and its promise of miracles take me back to my childhood, about which I am so equivocal, like everybody else. That means when I look into St. Joseph's Oratory, I am left with a dark, sinful intimation of swallowing. Yet I went there one day.

I was sitting at the bus stop outside the office of my gynecologist, one of a series of gynecologists who had added his notations to the file that followed me from city to city. He said they had done as much as they could, and I probably would not have children. I sat on the bench not knowing what to do. I did not want to return to our ugly apartment, and I could not reach Kim. Then an old man sat down beside me, and began to pop leaves. He was a sly-looking, rural old Québécois whose features all turned down. And what he did was, he picked leaves from the bushes behind us and examined them for holes. If they had none, he balled his left fist into an acoustic box, leaving it slightly open but curled. Then he put the leaf on top, on his index finger and thumb, and brought his right hand down flat to explode it with a popping sound. After that he looked up to see if I would ask him how he did it. But I didn't. I found I was no longer interested in the discreet miracles of daily life. I was horrified with myself, but I wanted to go to the Oratory and petition Brother André.

I knew I stood on the edge of vulgarity. On the bus, all the way around the mountain, I tried to think how I should appeal. I had to keep it ironic, self-deprecatory, guarded enough so that if I did get pregnant, there would be no unmistakable *quid pro quo,* and I would not have to embarrass myself by advertising a miracle to my friends. Behind this, however, was a thrumming beat of anger at Kim. I wanted to know where he was when I needed him. I wanted to tell him I was sick to death of this parade from city to city, from job to job, in search of some uplifting and so elusive meaning in my life. I wanted to get it secondhand, like everyone else, in a child. But mostly I was angry because I knew Kim would not miss having children. He was so impoverished. I wanted more. Than him. But the prayer to Brother André would not come, even when I found myself at the top of the stairs, looking into the Oratory. I nearly turned and went back down. But hopelessly, rather recklessly, I plunged in.

A corridor. On both sides, candles smouldered under dim religious paintings. There were pillars nailed with wooden crutches oiled so smooth they seemed antique. I saw no modern metal ones and almost hoped that Brother André had stopped his cures. I felt disconnected and out of place among the Catholic families who pressed by me. Perhaps I should have left, but I was held by some central doggedness: still the little girl who thought that when you started a book, you had to finish it. I read all of James Joyce's *Ulysses* when I was twelve years old, having taken it out of the library by mistake because I loved Greek myths. I always remembered how Leopold Bloom kept his hand in his pocket at the beach while he watched the pretty lady, although I understood that no more than the rest until I was sixteen, and realized what had happened in an embarrassed, congratulatory burst of sympathy: the kind I expected to feel here, should Brother André speak.

If speaking was the rule, I realized I did not know the Catholic formulae, and sharpened my wandering into a patrol to watch the way people knelt and crossed themselves: up, down, left-right, with their hands half-closed like small birds nestled there. Many knelt murmuring below a portrait of Brother André. They were mostly old, mostly women, with faint Mediterranean moustaches. I saw with almost hysterical clarity that I was utterly unlike them. I was so self-contained, so naïve, so Protestant. My hopes were not resonant with religion and family. I was more like the sad people who believed in tabloid newspapers. When I realized this, I *knew* I had to flee. Yet for some reason I do not know, I threw myself down and crossed myself casually. Then found it in me to pray. Dear Lord, you have made me an ordinary woman. Grant me the ordinary balm of a child.

I could have made one of my more successful stories out of this and told it to Kim over dinner. I could have bargained away my dignity for his belated attention. But I told him about neither the visit nor the doctor's conclusion. I was afraid he would mention adoption, when all I wanted in the world was my miracle. I had convinced myself that my unexpected sincerity made me deserve one. But I did not get pregnant, and grew vindictive instead. In Toronto, where we moved next, I could not get a job and refused to develop another convenient interest. Instead I phoned Kim at work to berate him about his hours, his preoccupation, about sex. I said his exhausted lovemaking kept us from having a child. I was that unfair. Sometimes I even tried to make the poor vain man cry, and when he did, his skin went blotched. Finally I couldn't stand myself anymore, and simply packed my bags and left. In another time, when separation was less possible, I think our marriage would have held together well enough. I would have been grateful to Kim for not wanting to have children, and found my peace in subservience. Perhaps we would have travelled, and given the neighbourhood children the foreign change we brought back. I would have taken a tolerant and tolerated interest in my nieces and nephews. Patronized charities; later, found a career. Because the truth is, our marriage was not impossible. Kim was terribly sorry I was unhappy.

3

Three men have been important in my life. Kim, of course, my father, and lately Greg, with whom I now live. Greg is a small man, some might say scrawny, but he drives a huge Detroit convertible and packs a big bag of pictures of his friends. When I am with him, I sometimes peer around to see if someone will rescue me from this queer mistake, preferably someone I don't know, or know well enough; say, Kim. The rest of the time I am laughing. Who would guess there is so much to laugh at in this world? Country music, the covers of early paperbacks, shinnying up a wall to put an "x" in the Marist convent sign. He is an organizer for a labour union; someone from the sixties who actually believes all those slogans. He tried to organize the bank where I used to work, and likes me because I do not try to organize him.

Eventually it was time to introduce Greg to my parents. They had retired to Florida, to a subdivision in the Keys. Greg wanted to drive straight down, so by the time we pulled up, he had eyes something like Rasputin. My father was poking in the tropical plants that grew around a palmetto, but when he recognized me, he straightened up and smiled shyly. My mother came bustling around the side of the house, calling, "Hello, hello." The old contrast had become exaggerated. My father just stood there with his arms hanging loose, as if they, he, were useless somehow, and I lost what I had to say to him. But my mother seemed to have redoubled her angry energy. After a cool look at Greg, she started slinging bags out of the car and telling us how tired we were, how bad the drive was, the humidity. She took me inside with the first load of luggage to show me what the humidity did to her fridge. The top was pocked and rusted from condensation.

"You'll find your father doesn't talk any more," she said abruptly. I turned and found her lounging against the counter. It would have been possible to mistake her attitude for self-satisfaction. I must have looked puzzled. She repeated, "He's decided not to speak."

"Will he write me a note?" I asked foolishly.

"He will not." Then, "You see what I have to put up with?" Her sudden self-pity embarrassed me, and made me feel defensive. She was talking about my father. I ducked and looked unhappily around the kitchen, which I could have picked out of any ten as the one belonging to my mother. She had always liked clean lines. Scandinavian modern: sometimes I felt she wanted to smooth me into mediocrity. I had always been closer to my father.

"Yes and no," I answered her unhappily.

"Yes and no," she agreed, and surprised me with a shrewd, older, dismissive look, as I once more ducked away.

The back of the house looked onto a canal with high concrete sides that reminded me somehow of dental work. Moored there was a small, adamantly one-man sailboat my mother said my father took out most days, and a beautiful old wooden cabin cruiser that Greg immediately coveted. He and my father went out the patio doors, my father nodding absently while Greg chattered. I watched them from the patio, Greg clambering aboard, my father stepping. I had wanted them to like each other, but I no longer saw how this could be possible.

"What do you suppose happened?" I asked Greg that night. He paused for a moment.

"Maybe a small stroke. My grandfather had one." I could not believe that.

"Then why would my mother have complained?"

"You're so hung up on cause and effect," he replied. "What happens isn't necessarily deserved."

We were there for only a few days, so my mother planned to make the most of it. The next morning we went out in the cabin cruiser, heading for a reef beyond Key West where we could go snorkelling. My mother sat aft, her legs crossed in white pants, her hair held back in a blue-and-white kerchief. She had thrown the snorkels and face-masks into the boat, then untied us casually and competently and pushed off. I had not seen her since their retirement, and found I had been expecting everyone's nervous, ageing mother, although the only reason I can give is that I had not really noticed her before. In fact this was a logical growth from the woman who had packed my lunch neatly every day, who mowed our huge lawn, comforted (how?) our neighbour. My father, however, seemed lopped, cut off. As he stood at the wheel, his arms looked useful now, if ropy, but the smile beneath his white captain's hat was too constant and forgetful, like a tic. He was not even in the same universe as Greg, who launched himself back and forth across the boat, taking pictures and exclaiming at the clear leafy colour of the water. The sky was a far faint blue. It seemed fainter than the vivid water as we chugged along the Keys, following the charts and buoys to make it through the shallows. Mangrove trees wove into islands in toward shore; little bug-sized cars scooted past on bridges. If Greg could have kept quiet, it would have been a perfect day, level and warm. There would have been nothing to silhouette my father's undemanding silence.

We reached the reef near mid-morning. The water had turned deep evening blue—the Gulf Stream, my mother said—then light again, weak as weak tea in its transparency. Through it now you could see brain coral, looking convoluted and clinical on top of the reef. There were dim clicking fish; sponges, dark and discarded looking on the sandy floor. My father mostly worked to hold our course, but once he glanced over shyly to see if I enjoyed it. When I smiled, he began to fumble with a wicker basket at his feet. My mother watched him absently as he pulled out packages of flavoured popcorn and tore them open—one hand on the wheel, one on the packages—using his teeth.

"For the fish," my mother said. "They're junk-food junkies." Only then did she go forward and take the wheel from my father, so he could step past her and start to throw popcorn in the water with straight, stiff sweeps of his arm. For a moment there was nothing. Then a few bright fish snapped off to starboard.

"Yellowtails," my mother called. "There'll be a school of

them." And she was right, more came; small silvery fish with spreading yellow tails. Greg whooped in excitement while my father grinned silently, and flung popcorn with his awkward arms. Soon the water itself was silver. The fish thrashed and snipped at the food, leaping on and over each other until the sea foamed like a waterfall. Greg couldn't get enough. He hollered out and snapped his pictures, then did a dance across the boat to my father. He clapped my father's back, twice, hard.

"Good work," he called. "Good work." My father laughed silently and shyly under Greg's arm. I wished that I could hug him too. I had held back, wanting to touch him but afraid I might be too delicate, or pitying or probing; afraid he might take it as forgiveness long past the time I think children have anything to forgive their parents for. But I was glad Greg could hug him. I had hoped a partner could make the connection with my family it is hard for me to make, across the distance I had negotiated to my independence. I grinned at my father, from one remove; even at my mother, while the fish flashed and flew upward, as silver, white and sparkling as winter breath above the shallow turquoise sea.

My father never did talk during our visit. Our closeness worked no miracle, except perhaps that I found myself temporarily adult enough to realize that if one did occur, we would not necessarily recognize it: the possibilities of life are so various and grand. Yet something did happen, that day on the ocean. As we ate, and rested, and swam, then chugged back up the keys, I looked at the ocean on one side and the subdivisions on the other, and saw that one was really no less monotonous than the other. Yet that had not stopped marvellous creatures from growing out of the sea. For a while, I lost my fear that my background had condemned me to be merely ordinary and expendable, although I am not claiming this made me any less so, or that the fear has not returned. I play with these ideas still—my mediocrity, and miracles—because of course the two are connected. I think miracles are an assurance, if they do occur, that we are not expendable, but rather part of some wondrous, directed scheme that allows us honour and individuality, and promises that it will continue after this life. The lack of them says simply, to me, that we will endure no more than a leaf or a flower. Sometimes I can accept that. Sometimes I look around at the beauty of life in this world and I think it is sufficient. But sometimes it is not, and I pray.